Time for a Party

Tim Daviason

Stephen Morris

The persons and events in this book are entirely fictious;

no depiction of persons living or dead is intended.

First published in 2021 by Stephen Morris

www.stephen-morris.co.uk smc@freeuk.com

ISBN 978-1-9160953-9-7
British Library Cataloguing-in-Publication Data
A catalogue record for this book is available from the British Library

1

It was on a Saturday, a few days before we were due to fly out to Nice, that I first became aware that my Cousin Clara had written a book. In fact, I knew very little about Clara beyond the fact that she was a distant cousin and had died when I was still a child.

I hardly need to say that I enjoy Saturday mornings. No need to keep checking the time, no need to down a coffee in a few quick gulps, no need to rush off to beat the traffic - instead, a leisurely breakfast followed by a gentle stroll to the village corner shop to buy the newspaper, and a day to look forward to without haste, hassle or hurry.

 I drew back the bedroom curtains just a little so as not to wake my wife Charlotte but enough to reveal a sunny day and a cloudless blue sky. Spirits up another notch or two.

We live, my wife and I and Plato the cat, in a seventeenth-century cottage with mullioned windows and Cotswold stone walls on the outskirts of a pretty village called Cloverton, about an hour's drive south of Birmingham where I work as a public relations and marketing consultant.

I lingered a moment or two at the window before returning to bed again. I never tire of the view: of distant hills rising beyond a patchwork of fields with the occasional old farm building and in the foreground across the lane from our cottage, a traditional wild flower meadow, haven to many species of birds and butterflies; a view neither dramatic nor spectacular but of a quintessentially English, unassuming beauty.

Our Cottage stands in an elevated position half way along a quiet lane leading from the fourteenth-century village church of St. Barnabas to Cloverton Hall, an Elizabethan manor with its characteristic forest of tall chimneys and domed turrets.

I often congratulated myself on my decision…well, to be absolutely fair, *our* decision, that is to say Charlotte and I … to purchase the cottage. We had been on the point of signing up to buy a perfectly nice terraced house in a respectable suburban district of Birmingham which in many ways would have been the *sensible* choice, but the cottage was unquestionably for us the *right* choice.

I was still in an uplifted sort of mood as I walked to the village…or perhaps I should say relatively uplifted. A few niggles, despite my efforts to ignore them, had managed to wriggle their way back into my consciousness. We all have our niggles, of course, some more niggly than others, but some people are much better than me at filing them away in some separate little compartment in their minds labelled 'things to worry about later but not today'.

There were two niggles, in particular, that were bothering me:

First, I had learnt that one of my better clients, a housebuilding company called Greenvale Homes, was in merger negotiations with a larger developer based in Manchester. The term 'merger' would almost certainly be a euphemism for a takeover by the Manchester company, and that might well mean the end of my profitable relationship with Greenvale. A bitter blow.

Secondly, I'd recently made quite a substantial investment for my personal pension plan in a unit trust fund. It had been highly rated and its fund manager was very well respected, a darling of the financial pundits. Shortly afterwards, however, I had read an article in the *FT* by a well-known economic journalist, who had expressed the view that the fund was too heavily biased towards investments in emerging economies – which were likely to suffer in the event of a global economic downturn. Ought I to sell?

"Come on Geoff," Charlotte had said to me just after I'd got home from work on the previous evening, "I can tell you're worried about something."

I can never hide anything from Charlotte. She knows me too well, so I confessed to the two niggling issues on my mind.

"I thought PR types like you were supposed to be sunny optimists. I'm sure everything will be okay."

"Well, it is true that PR types, as you put it, need to project a positive image, but that doesn't completely exempt us from life's worries and concerns. I do always, though, try to appear upbeat and reassuring in the presence of clients."

"But not always with me!"

"That's because you're my wife"

"Huh!"

***

Cloverton is quite a large village and unlike some of the smaller villages and hamlets nearby, it has not become simply a dormitory village for those who work in nearby towns and cities. It still has a life of its own.

The shop where I buy my newspaper, Cloverton Village Stores, occupies a corner of the village high street. As well as newspapers it stocks all the sort of things you would expect to find in a convenience store.

Next to the shop there used to be a bank; no more, sadly, nor any other bank branch in the village, only a solitary ATM. The former bank premises has been nicely converted into a thriving bakery and café.

Further along on the same side of the street are a greengrocer, a butcher's shop and an off licence and, on the other side, the village pub, The Black Swan, an estate agency, a florist, a pharmacy and a charity book shop.

Before heading for home I thought I'd have a quick browse in the charity shop. Most of the books sell for two or three pounds, but there was a shelf reserved for books of greater value, some of them brand new and some old. It was old books in which I was most interested. The prices tended to be rather higher, of course, but still good value and on occasion I'd managed to find a real bargain. Collecting old books is a hobby of mine.

I nearly missed it, but on a second sweep of the shelf, there it was – a book I simply had to buy.

It was entitled 'Time for a Party' by Clara Momford.

My surname, too, is Momford, and I recalled my father had once referred to a Clara Momford.

'A remote cousin of ours', he had said. 'A rather racy woman who used to live in the South of France and died when you were a young lad.'

It was a beautiful book in very good condition for its age. The binding was of red Moroccan leather and the cover design – very thirties in style – depicted a lady smoking a cigarette in a very long holder. The smoke from the cigarette curled sinuously upwards until it reached the title. The high quality paper made it a real pleasure to turn the pages.

Opening the book I found, after the flyleaf, a page with a dedication:

For my dear friends Margot and Louis

The next page contained a brief preface which read:

My dearest friend Clara Momford was a well-known socialite amongst the rich and fashionable elite gracing the French Riviera in the years between the wars. As a young woman she first worked in London at the War Office before settling in the South of France in 1923, where she had acquired a large pink mansion, Villa Mirabeau set in luxuriant gardens at Cap Ferrat.

The villa soon acquired a legendary status for the lavish parties which Clara hosted there. There were often rumours of scandalous goings-on and Clara, too, acquired something of a reputation as a femme fatale. This was not at all true but Clara quite shamelessly enjoyed playing up to the rôle. As she writes: 'I do so love to shock people and, however disapproving they pretend to be, everyone secretly loves to be shocked'. In any event, few ever turned down an invitation and Clara's beauty, wit and charm soon conquered everyone who met her.

Villa Mirabeau remained her home until April 1939 when, with war looming again in Europe, Clara returned to England where she became involved in charity work helping refugees.

This book was mostly written during her time in France but left in abeyance during the war years. A year or so after the end of the war, however, I finally managed to persuade her to finish it and seek a publisher.

She returned to France after the war for occasional visits but never again took up permanent residence. 'Darling,' she said to me. 'It simply wouldn't be the same. The world is a different place now'.

I should add that some of the characters – friends, lovers, party guests and others – who appear in this book are referred to only by their first names, pseudonyms or aliases to conceal their identity and spare their blushes.

Margot Bentham

London, July 1946

The author was indeed the very Clara Momford, the distant relative of whom my father had spoken.

There was another good reason, too, for me to buy the book. As I have already mentioned Charlotte and I were due shortly to fly to Nice. An old university friend of mine John and his wife Anna had invited us, as they kindly did almost every year, to stay with them at their lovely apartment in Villefranche-sur-Mer on the French Riviera. Villefranche is within walking distance of Cap Ferrat.

What could possibly make for a better holiday read?

The book was priced at £15.99, a snip, and without a second thought I paid up and left.

Delighted with my purchase, I set off for home at a brisk pace, my niggling worries for now at least entirely forgotten.

***

Charlotte was waiting for me in the hallway.

"Well, where are the lamb chops?" she asked.

"Lamb chops?"

"I asked you to get four lamb chops from the butchers' for our lunch."

"Ah, yes. Sorry, um, I forgot…but I did buy this wonderful book."

"Oh, really, Geoff, how could you forget?! You can't *eat* books, you know!"

"Well, you can't *read* lamb chops!"

Not for the first time that week, I was cast into *La maison des chiens*.

2

I owe my existence to a good lunch.

These were the words which began the first chapter of Clara's book and greeted my eyes after I had slipped into bed.

It was our first night at John and Anna's flat in Villefranche. It had been a long day and I must say I had been looking forward to bedtime.

Unlike Charlotte, however, who falls asleep within seconds of laying her head on the pillow I am unable to sleep without reading, at least for a short while, a process which as Prospero put it in The Tempest helps to 'still my beating mind'.

I had quizzed my father before leaving home as to whether he knew anything more about Clara.

"Not really." He said. "She came from another branch of the Momford family … remote cousins … lived somewhere in London … never met Clara or any of them for that matter … fell on hard times, I believe. There was some sort of scandal to do with Clara's mother. I remember old Aunt Alice, a mine of knowledge about our family history, talking about it but I can't now recall exactly what it was all about."

Since old Aunt Alice had been dead for over twenty years that wasn't of much further use, but I had also done a bit of research on the internet and found a reference to Clara in a piece about the Jazz Age in the South of France. It said much the same things as the preface to Clara's book but not a lot beyond that save to record that Clara had died in London in 1979.

I continued to read:

My father, Charles, was the scion of a wealthy banking family. His own father was the chairman of the family-owned private bank with offices in the City of London. Charles had just been appointed as a junior director and my Mother Grace Momford was employed as his secretary. She was just twenty-years old and it was her first real job.

Grace also came from a good family but her father Kenneth Momford a kind but gullible man, had ill-advisedly frittered away the bulk of the family fortune on a variety of dubious overseas investments, all offering very high returns but all, of course, ultimately disastrous. The family only survived by taking in lodgers.

Charles was engaged to be married to an eminently suitable but rather dull girl from an old and respected family whose father was currently the Master of a venerable City livery company.

Grace had no romantic attachments at the time but to keep up with her friends was desperate to have one.

Charles was an extremely good-looking man and Grace was a very pretty young woman of a shy but charming demeanour. They were instantly attracted to one another. It may not have been love at first sight on Monday, the first day of her engagement at the bank, but it was certainly love by close of business on Friday. Of course neither expressed their true feelings, Charles being a man of a reserved nature not to mention one engaged to be married; and my mother too awestruck, shy and confused. So initially nothing passed between them other than an occasional furtive glance.

And so things might have remained: feelings bottled up, words unspoken, nothing beyond the formal and proper relationship between an employer and a member of his staff.

However, one day Charles was invited to lunch by his Uncle Eustace at one of the grander London clubs. Unlike Charles' father, a quiet abstemious man, Uncle Eustace was a loud, flamboyant character, a bon viveur who treated his nephew to a splendid meal. Each course was accompanied with superb wines selected from the club's extensive wine list. In fact it would be more accurate to say that the food accompanied the wine than the other way round. Never before had Charles been wined and dined, especially wined, in such a lavish manner.

When Charles returned to the bank he called Grace to his office where she encountered a quite different sort of man to the one which she knew as her employer. Gone was the diffident, polite Charles to be replaced by a man red in the face, swaying slightly from side to side and slurring his words.

"That'sh a vair pretty dressh you wearing, Grace…a pretty dressh for a vair, vair pretty girl!"

"Oh, thank you, sir," mother had replied, blushing profusely.

With that, Charles lurched towards her, and with an arm around her waist, kissed her ardently on the lips.

My mother should have pushed him away if not slapped his face, but she didn't. She was like the peasant girl, Zerlina, lured by Don Giovanni in the famous seduction duet 'La ci darem la mano' in my favourite Mozart opera. 'Vorrei e non vorrei' Zerlina sings, 'I want to and I don't want to' – a line that precisely reflected the ambivalence of my mother's feelings towards Charles. For my mother like the hapless Zerlina, the temptation in the end proved too great. She gave way to it.

A trickle became a stream, a stream became a flood, a flood became a raging torrent of desire … a mutual passion satisfied as they sprawled together on the Turkish rug laid on the floor of Charles' office amidst piles of debenture deeds, company prospectuses, bond certificates and mortgage securities.

The next morning my father, his normal reserved self now restored, was mortified. He was ashamed, entirely to blame he said, for what had happened and yet my mother could not possibly remain with the bank, let alone as his secretary. He had arranged for her to be taken on by a stockbroker friend at an equivalent salary.

Tearfully, my mother departed.

That might have been an end of the matter, but it wasn't.

A short while later she discovered to her horror, that she was pregnant.

I turned the page keen to read more, but I could barely keep my eyes open as sleep finally crept up on me. I would just have to wait till morning to learn what happened next.

3

I awoke as a thin pencil of light penetrated a gap between two of the upper wooden slats of the shutter blind. Hauling myself out of bed I tiptoed to the bathroom as quietly as I could so as not to wake Charlotte, dressed and made my way through the French windows of the salon out onto the terrace. There was just enough room there for four chairs and a small table but it had a great view of the bay, part of the old town and along the coast to Cap Ferrat.

Though still early it was already quite warm. Nobody else in the flat had yet stirred. I settled myself in one of chairs and began to read Clara's book from where I'd left off.

Perhaps finding it emotionally difficult to dwell too much on this episode, she dealt fairly briefly with the events which followed the discovery of her mother's pregnancy:

> There had been discreet discussions between the two families. Nobody, of course, wanted a scandal. Charles' family, who were clearly most anxious that the 'suitable but dull' fiancée and her family should hear nothing of this unfortunate affair, agreed to pay a generous monthly allowance to my mother from the date she needed to give up work until her future well-being could be secured.

> It was arranged that I would be adopted.

> An approach had been made to a couple, Mr. & Mrs. Leonard Parfitt, with whom there was a family connection and who had been unable to have children of their own. They were delighted to have the opportunity to adopt a baby and their absolute discretion as to the circumstances leading to the adoption could be entirely relied upon. Until the mid-1920s there was in fact no formal statutory procedure for adoption in Britain so legally I was a foster-child but the Parfitts would always treat me as if I were their own daughter.

> I was born, a healthy baby, on the 21st June 1895.

Leonard Parfitt was a civil servant and his wife, Helena, busied herself with good works for various charitable causes. They may not have been quite as rich as Charles' parents but they were certainly wealthy, well-to-do folk with a beautiful home overlooking the River Thames at Richmond, where I was brought up.

Charles, my actual father, paid occasional visits to see me as I grew up and was always referred to as 'Uncle Charles'. I never met my grandparents and only met my mother, Grace, much later.

Clara summed matters up in the final paragraph of the chapter:

During my childhood and school days I knew nothing of my origins. So far as I was concerned I was a young girl living in a comfortable home with two loving parents and my name was Clara Parfitt. I only discovered on my seventeenth birthday that I was adopted and it was only then that I saw my birth certificate for the first time. It showed that my mother was Grace Momford; my father's name was not recorded. The certificate simply stated "Father unknown" – untrue, but no doubt part of the bargain struck between the families. A bargain about me in which I had no say.

Even then I had no knowledge of the full circumstances surrounding my arrival in the world until I finally met Grace, the mother who gave birth to me, in the Spring of 1922 some three and a half years after the end of the Great War. But that is a story for another chapter.

I cannot blame Charles and Grace for their conduct. Indeed, it would be hypocritical of me to do so in the light of the life I have led. They may be my real parents but Leonard and Helena Parfitt would always be my true parents, the ones who loved me and gave me a home.

I continued to call myself 'Parfitt' until I decided to settle in France when I changed my name to Momford. I never told the Parfitts of the change and to them I always remained Clara Parfitt. I was Parfitt in England, Momford in France.

I was about to continue with the next chapter when I heard the first noises of stirring within the flat. Someone else was now awake and a short while later John appeared at my elbow with a cup of coffee for me.

"Been here long?" he asked.

"Well, for a little while. I like to get up early as you know. It's the best time of day."

"I doubt that our wives would agree."

"Probably not." I had to admit.

"How are you getting along with the book by the way?"

"Well, I've managed a couple of chapters so far."

"Any scandals, skeletons in the cupboard?"

"Well, one at least."

"Oh good! Every family worth its salt should have a skeleton or two in the ancestral cupboard, and I'm sure yours is no exception. Makes life more interesting."

"I'm sure there'll be some more scandals to come, particularly when I get to the wild parties Clara is supposed to have hosted at her villa."

"Let's hope so. You must tell me all about it. By the way, Anna's going out to get some fresh croissants," John said changing the subject. "Breakfast should soon be on the way."

***

After breakfast on the terrace the rest of the day, our first full day in France, was spent not doing very much apart from a walk around the old town, up to the castle on the hill, and a bit of shopping.

Before setting out for our walk I checked my phone for emails and, amongst the usual dross, found two very reassuring ones:

One was from my secretary keeping me up to date with work matters. She also added that she'd had a call from the sales director of Greenvale who had told her, off the record, that the merger negotiations had fallen through.

The second came from my broker who advised that I shouldn't be too concerned about the report in the *FT*. The journalist concerned was alone in his opinion. Others had expressed a quite different view and, since my purchase the value of the units had continued to rise.

I hastened to tell Charlotte the cheering news.

"There you are then," she said. "Your trouble is that you always worry about things that will probably never happen."

I was not, however, to be free from niggles for long. There was another giant worry just waiting to catch me rudely by surprise

***

Instead of going to a restaurant the plan was to have supper in the flat that evening, which the girls would prepare together while John and I went out for a pre-prandial glass or two at our favourite bar on the sea front.

I was in a more relaxed mood when John and I returned. I felt I'd finally managed to slip into holiday mode.

"Come on you two," Anna called out. "Supper's ready."

As the first course, a traditional salad Niçoise, was produced John opened an impressive-looking, unusually shaped bottle of rosé which he assured us came from one of the very best wineries in Provence.

John is a thoroughly good bloke and this was a kind gesture, but he sometimes gets carried away with his interest in fine wines. He proceeded to describe the very *special specialness* of the wine in exhaustive detail, even how the grapes were picked (during the night apparently) and with that mind-numbing enthusiasm which seems to be the particular preserve of wine bores. One often hears the expression 'infectious enthusiasm'. All I can say is that I hope I never catch a dose of it. Mind you,

Charlotte often accuses me of being obsessed with collecting rare books and I dare say that someone droning on at dinner parties about books on obscure topics which nobody has ever read, by authors of whom they've never heard, might be rather boring too.

We'd only just finished with the salad Niçoise and Anna had proudly ferried in the main course – a Provençal lamb stew with olives and a side dish of Ratatouille – when I got a call on my mobile and went out onto the terrace where the signal was better.

It was Donald Watson, a solicitor by profession and a friend and neighbour of ours back home in Cloverton.

"Hello, Donald," I answered. "Nice to hear from you."

"I'm not sure that 'nice' is quite the word, Geoff. I'm afraid I've got some rather bad news."

"Oh, dear. What's that?"

"Lord Pendlebury has just submitted applications for planning permission and listed building to convert Cloverton Hall into a wedding venue and conference centre along with various alterations and additions to provide for extra guest accommodation and other services."

Lawrence Pendlebury had inherited on the death of his father, George about a year before, both the family's hereditary title and ownership of the Hall. I had not yet met him; he and his wife had since his father's demise kept themselves to themselves, without much contact with the village. This awful proposal came right out of the blue.

"Oh, Christ!" I said. "If this gets permission…God forbid, it would mean hundreds of people, noisy wedding receptions some probably going on through the night, traffic congestion and God knows what else besides. It would transform the village, especially our end of it – and not at all in a good way!"

"Worse still," Donald added, "the application includes a proposal to convert most of the wild flower meadow which forms part of the Cloverton Hall estate opposite our houses, into a car park for wedding guests and conference delegates. Only a token area near the church would be preserved."

"Holy shit!"

"Yes, couldn't be worse, could it?"

"I can't believe that the planning authority would ever permit this, would they?"

"Well, I wouldn't be too sure of that. It's certainly not my view, but there is an argument that it would create employment opportunities and boost trade in the area."

"Well, we must all do everything possible to oppose this thing."

"I agree and I'm trying to get together a committee of local people to co-ordinate objections, lobby local councillors and so on. I wonder if you would be prepared to join? Your PR experience would be very useful."

"Sure thing. Count me in. I'll do whatever I can as soon as I'm back home. In the meantime, do please keep me informed."

"Will do. See you when you're back, Geoff. Bye for now."

***

I suppose 'ashen-faced' has become a rather overworked expression but that's how I must have looked when I returned to the table.

"What on earth's the matter, Geoff?" Charlotte asked. "You look as though you've seen a ghost."

I did my best to explain the situation. There were sharp intakes of breath. Everyone seemed quite as shocked by the news as I was.

"I think I'd better open another bottle," John said, to unanimous approval.

***

Later, as Charlotte and I prepared for bed she gave me one of her special looks, the sort of half-smile with head tilted to one side look which a kindly nurse might give a nervous patient to calm him down before being wheeled off to the operating theatre.

"Look, Geoff, I know you're worried about this Cloverton Hall thing. So am I for that matter, but there's not much we can do about it here, not till we get back home, is there? "There's no point," she said, ever practical as she was, "in letting it spoil our holiday."

"You're quite right," I said. "I'll do my best not to think too much about it."

But that, of course, was easier said than done.

4

Unable to sleep I took myself off to the salon (as John liked to call it) and tried to distract myself with reading a little more of Clara's book.

Clara dealt with her childhood and early life quite economically, in fact in just one chapter. Her life with the Parfitts and her schooldays were described a little blandly as:

> …a wonderful time passed in idyllic surroundings.

I suppose it was the life of any young girl of a privileged background from a comfortable home might have enjoyed at that time. Clara may have thought there would have been nothing much to interest readers. I suspect the main reason, however, was that she wanted to get on to writing about the sixteen years or so of her life in France. In fact in Margot Bentham's preface it is clear that her time in the South of France was intended to be the principal focus of the book.

There were, however, one or two incidents in her early life which she described in greater detail, notably her first sexual encounter.

> Girls in those days, of course, were brought up, as I was, to be chaste and pure of thought and most were, poor things, but I was an exception. My upbringing utterly failed in this respect and my parents would have been horrified if they had known of my sexual thoughts and yearnings.

The trouble was that contact with boys was strictly controlled and Clara's desire to lose her virginity was unsurprisingly frustrated, but she eventually achieved her ambition on her nineteenth birthday. She expresses her view on the matter in characteristic manner:

I have always thoroughly detested the expression 'loss of virginity' as if it were like losing an umbrella and even more so I hate it when people talk of a girl 'being de-flowered' as if it were a process akin to dead-heading a rose bush. Surely one's first experience of sex should be a gain not a loss, a blossoming not a de-flowering.

Malcolm was the name of the young man responsible for the de-flowering – or rather blossoming. He was the son of wealthy parents. They were close neighbours and friends of the Parfitts and lived in an even grander house, a mansion indeed. Clara and Malcolm were instantly attracted to one another in the same way that Charles and her mother had been. With a little subtle prompting from Clara, Malcolm overcame his shyness enough to persuade his parents to invite Clara for tea to celebrate her nineteenth birthday. The plan was that when tea was over Malcom would ask Clara if she would like to go for a walk in the garden to see the carp pond. The garden was extensive, and the pond well out of sight of the drawing room window.

Poor Malcom was very nervous and I had consumed two chocolate éclairs and a slice of ginger cake before he steeled himself to stammer out the planned invitation to show me the carp pond.

His mother thought this an excellent suggestion and we set out across the wide croquet lawn and thence via the rose alley to the famous carp pond. There were in fact no carp to be seen. They were no doubt skulking beneath the water lilies, taking a well-earned rest from their daily routine of swimming very slowly round and round in circles.

Beyond the pond was an extensive laurel hedge immediately behind which through a small iron gate, a path led to the kitchen garden. Here on one side stood a large greenhouse of a rather peculiar gothic design and on the other side a substantial garden shed half-shielded by a row of apple trees. It was to the latter edifice that Malcom led me. He had earlier thoughtfully smuggled from the house a small rug to lay on the hard-wooden floor inside the shed upon which it was intended that we should consummate our mutual passion.

My mother had lost her innocence on a rug on the floor of a banker's office and so I too lost mine on a rug – one laid on the floor of a garden shed between a wheelbarrow, a spade and a pitchfork. In truth I was very glad to be rid of it. What use is innocence, after all in a wicked world? I suppose that a garden shed was not the most romantic place for one's first proper sexual experience but at least the rug was a fine Persian Baluchi!

Clara continued to see Malcolm regularly thereafter. They had become what we would call today 'an item'. Mr. and Mrs. Parfitt were delighted. Malcolm's parents were good friends; they thought that Malcolm was an eminently suitable young man and quietly encouraged the relationship.

Of course, they knew nothing of the happy discarding of my innocence.

Clara's romance with Malcolm had begun in 1914, that most fateful of years. In August Britain declared war on Germany as a result of her invasion of Belgium and the subsequent refusal to remove her troops from Belgian soil. Malcolm signed up and only a few months later was killed at the first battle of the Marne.

I cried and cried for days on end. I do truly believe that Malcolm and I might in due course have become man and wife and, who knows, I might have taken up flower arrangement and become a respectable woman.

I managed to read on to the end of the chapter but suddenly began to feel drowsy. I don't remember making my way back to bed but I woke up there, having suffered an appalling nightmare in which thousands of cars were crammed into the once lovely meadow opposite our home, now gravelled over with dreary brown grit. More cars were queuing to drive into the park, but there was no room for them. It seemed that I had become a car park attendant and was trying to turn the cars back. They kept coming, revving their engines and hooting angrily as they came. A large, ugly woman in a bridal gown and veil shouted at me: *You silly little man, don't you realise it's my wedding day. You must let me into the park. You must…You must!*

This whole disturbing nightmare lingered in my mind even after I'd woken up; it was only after I had made my way to the terrace that I was able to shake it off.

I sat to watch the gorgeous spectacle as the sun came up over the bay until it was light enough for me to continue with Clara's book.

The next chapter concerned her life during the years of the Great War and thereafter to June 1923, some nine years. Again, this period of her life was dealt with briefly, in a mere twenty-three pages with only a few incidents of some importance described in greater detail.

She had told her parents, that is to say the Parfitts, that she would like to do something to aid the war effort, feeling that she owed it to the memory of her dear Malcolm. So it was arranged that she would work as a land girl on a farm in Kent. The farmer was a tenant of Helena Parfitt's brother who owned a large farm near Canterbury. It was thought that mixing with other land girls from a different background would broaden Clara's mind and that life on the farm would be good for her.

It was not a success.

The other girls plainly thought her snooty, an accusation to which she readily admits and further, as she puts it:

> I was obviously not born to dig for potatoes in a muddy field.

Some while later through the good offices and influence of Leonard Parfitt, himself a senior civil servant, employment was found for her as a junior secretary at the War Office. This was much more to her liking.

After the war she continued to work at the War Office, moving up a few grades to a more senior position and, it was there in 1919, that she met another girl who came to work there. This was Margot Bentham, who became a life-long friend and who would one day write the preface to her book.

Margot and I were about the same age. We shared everything together: our thoughts and feelings, our secrets, our love of food, wine and fun, and later, quite often, our lovers. We were two of a kind.

Margot lived with her parents in a magnificent house in Cheyne Walk by the Thames in Chelsea. (Indeed, it seemed to me that all Clara's early friends or their parents were, almost without exception, enormously wealthy and lived in beautiful houses or mansions and invariably within sight of or close to the Thames.)

Margot suggested that Clara might like to come and live at Cheyne Walk during the working week, an arrangement with which Margot's parents – Sir Henry Bentham, a retired diplomat, and his wife Lady Fiona Bentham – were apparently very happy and indeed encouraged. Clara was of course only too delighted to accept this kind offer.

So, from 1919 to 1923 Clara lived during the week in Chelsea, sharing a bedroom with Margot, and at weekends returned to her family home in Richmond.

One day in April 1922, quite out of the blue Clara received a letter from Grace, her biological mother whom she'd never met.

In the letter Grace invited Clara for tea at Claridges where she was staying. Initially, Clara was reluctant to accept the invitation. Why would she want to meet the mother who had given her up for adoption? In the end, however, curiosity got the better of her and she accepted.

Grace's shy charm, which had so attracted Charles, had been replaced by a wry worldliness.

As I munched my way through a plate of cucumber sandwiches, she gave me the fullest account of the circumstances surrounding my far from immaculate conception, sparing me not the smallest detail however embarrassing. She spoke in a breezy, matter-of-fact sort of way and though I tried to maintain a serious composure, I was unable to resist the occasional giggle. In fact we both giggled.

It had been terrible, she said, to give me up for adoption but there had been no option at the time and she was sure that I would have had a happy childhood with the Parfitts and would have wanted for nothing.

I asked how she had known where to write to me with her invitation. Much to my surprise she told me that she had been in regular touch with Charles, 'Uncle Charles' as I still called him despite the truth of the matter.

Why then, I asked, had she not come to see me before?

First of all, she felt that any such approach might have upset the Parfitts but, more to the point, she had been living abroad for many years in America.

After leaving the bank, she had spent the next five years working for the firm of stockbrokers where Charles had arranged employment for her. It was here that she had met Royston Garfield Jnr, an American from a family of wealthy industrialists in the steel business based in Chicago. Royston was a client of the firm which advised upon his and his company's investments in Britain. He had only spoken to Grace a few times on the telephone and met her once at the stockbrokers' offices, but he was immediately taken with her in much the same way as Charles had been. It didn't, however, need the stimulus of a good lunch with a surfeit of fine wines for him to make an advance. Indeed he invited her to join him for dinner at Brown's Hotel on the very evening of their first meeting.

After a whirlwind affair Grace, swept off her feet, accepted his proposal of marriage.

Royston was a widower in his forties with two teenage children. Though much older than Grace, they shared many interests. It was a happy marriage, their time divided between New York and Chicago, mainly Chicago, where they lived in sumptuous splendour at a grand baronial mansion in a prime position on Lake Shore Drive. Much to their mutual regret there were no children of their marriage and sadly in October 1921, the year before Grace's visit to Britain, Royston died of a heart attack. He left an enormous fortune which under the terms of his Will was divided one half equally between the two children of his former marriage and the remainder for Grace. As a consequence Grace was now an immensely wealthy woman.

I saw her several times more before she returned to America and I accompanied her to Liverpool where, with tears in my eyes, I watched as she boarded the liner *Franconia* bound for New York.

I suppose it was partly meeting my mother that would lead me eventually to adopt the name Momford. It was not just that Grace was my natural mother and her name was the only surname on my birth certificate (my father being 'unknown'); not just that I was perfectly entitled to take it; there was more to it than that. It was not quite like my close friendship with Margot – there was the generational difference between my mother and I and great differences between the circumstances of our lives – but there had grown up between us an immediate and special feeling of affection and understanding.

It was only two weeks or so after Grace's return to America that Clara and Margot travelled by train to the South of France, to stay with Margot's parents at their beautiful bougainvillea-clad villa in the hills above Menton, near the Italian border.

One day they were all invited to lunch by friends of Lady Bentham who lived near St Jean de Cap Ferrat. The Benthams had acquired a motor car, a brand new Delage, to keep at the villa for use during their visits and it was in this splendid vehicle with Sir Henry himself at the wheel, that they made the short journey from Menton to Cap Ferrat.

As they left St Jean on the way to Lady Bentham's friends' home further up the Cap, they took a wrong turning and found themselves in a short cul-de-sac at the end of which was a large villa. A sign on the gatepost in just-legible white letters declared this to be *Villa Mirabeau;* a notice had been attached to the rusty iron gate. *A Vendre* it read: for sale.

The villa had pink plastered walls and green shutters. The place had obviously seen better days. It looked to Clara as if it had been unoccupied for some time and there was an air of general decay and dilapidation about it. The paintwork of both walls and shutters was faded and peeling and there were cracks in the walls and broken guttering. The short driveway had deep potholes and the garden had become a jungle. Nevertheless, she fell instantly in love with it.

As I looked at the villa, I experienced a sudden and quite uncanny feeling that it was somehow calling out to me:

'Please, please rescue me from ruin, bring me back to life, come and live with me'.

It was extraordinary but without any doubt in my mind I knew at that very moment that this is where I wanted to be; this is where I belonged. And it was for sale too. But how could I ever think of buying it and living there? I had no money to speak of. It was an impossible dream.

As the car reversed down the short lane, Rue Mirabeau, I looked back longingly at the villa as if I was leaving an old friend whom I might never see again. Back on the main road it didn't take too long to find the house where we had been invited to lunch and which was close by. It proved to be another lovely old villa, not unlike the Villa Mirabeau but in pristine condition.

Lunch was taken on a wide terrace shaded from the sun by a wooden canopy entwined with a mix of honeysuckle and grapevines. A long table stretched almost the length of the terrace with chairs and place settings for at least twenty guests. This was not the small gathering that I had imagined it would be but a much more formal affair with smartly dressed waiters and waitresses, hired for the occasion, to serve the food and pour the wines.

The terrace overlooked a well-kept garden with a wide lawn, bordered by palms and lush sub-tropical flora, sloping gently down to the rocky seashore beyond.

I found myself seated next to an exceptionally handsome, well-dressed man some years older than me. For the purposes of this book I will omit his surname and simply refer to him as Louis. Louis was half French, half English. His French father was a wealthy businessman, with interests in shipping and the wine trade. His mother was English. He spoke the language as fluently as he did French, having received his education so he told me, at Winchester and Oxford. Unlike the rest of his family his home was in Paris. He was, however, a frequent visitor to the south of France where he had business interests and many friends.

There are some people whom I sense at once to be kindred spirits, people with whom one establishes an immediate rapport and who I feel instinctively share the same thoughts and feelings without the need to express them in words. There are others, though, however agreeable they may be, with whom I know that I will never enjoy more than a pleasant casual acquaintance. Louis fell quite definitely into the former category.

Margot was seated on the other side of him, looking quite ravishing in the new summer frock her mother had bought for her at a fashionable shop just off the Place Massena in Nice. Even as a wayward hand gently caressed my thigh, I caught him turning his head to study Margot's trim figure, before he abruptly looked away to cast his eye over a pretty young waitress as she approached the table with a large tureen of Soupe des Rougets. So what if he was a bit of a rogue? I thought. I'm no angel after all. He was suave, charming, witty, ever so handsome and I liked him.

I told him of my silly dream regarding the Villa Mirabeau.

It appeared that he knew it well. It had been owned by a Parisian lawyer who had died before the war. His elderly widow, who had inherited, was in a nursing home and never came there. It had been advertised for sale for some years but its sorry condition deterred potential purchasers.

"My dear sweet Clara," he said, as if we were old lovers. "Of course Villa Mirabeau will be yours! It cries out for a person of your charm and radiant beauty to restore it to its former glory."

"But it's money I need to buy and restore it. I hardly have enough to buy a new summer dress, let alone a villa!"

"Fate will find a way my dearest, just you wait and see and then we, you and I together, shall throw such grand parties there that everyone who's anyone will beg for an invitation!"

With these prophetic words the chapter came to a close. That seemed to be a convenient point for me to break off, and I went to the kitchen to make myself a cup of coffee.

5

"Tell you what," I said to Charlotte as we got ourselves dressed next morning.

"What?"

"Well, unless you particularly want to go to St Paul de Vence with John and Anna today, we could go and see the villa."

"What villa?"

"The Villa Mirabeau of course, the one referred to in Clara's book."

"Do you know, I think that's quite a good idea."

"Well, I do have them occasionally… So you don't mind missing out on the trip to St Paul de Vence?"

"No, I don't mind a bit. It's a very pretty place but we've been there many times before."

"Good! Then we can set off after breakfast. I suggest we walk there. I think it would only take about forty-five minutes or so to reach St Jean de Cap Ferrat from here and perhaps another quarter of an hour or so from there to the villa. I've checked Google Maps for the exact location of the Rue Mirabeau and I think I know how to get there."

***

Just after leaving the flat with Charlotte I got a call on my mobile.

"Hello, Is that Mr. Momford?"

"Speaking."

"You won't know me. My name is Matthew Duncan. Mrs. Prout at the charity shop in Cloverton gave me your number."

"Oh, yes."

The redoubtable Mrs Prout, the local pharmacist's wife, was a volunteer at the charity shop and indeed had been there when I bought Clara's book. She was a member of the local book club to which I also belonged and had my mobile number. My immediate thought was that the call might have something to do with the club, but I was quite wrong.

"I'm so sorry to trouble you, but I believe you bought a book at the shop last Saturday"

"Yes. 'Time for a Party' by Clara Momford."

"That's the one. This is, umm, a bit embarrassing for me but my wife was helping me clear out a load of old books and other stuff at our cottage in Upper Cloverton and she mistakenly included the Momford book along with the dozen or so other ones which she took to the shop. And, well, the fact is I'd rather like it back."

"Oh dear!"

"You see it belonged originally to my grandfather who lived in Monte Carlo for most of his life except for the war years. He used to advise other ex-pats down on the Riviera with regard to their business and financial dealings including, so I believe, Clara Momford. I'm afraid the book's been languishing in a box in the attic for years and years. I've never read it and I doubt my father did either, but I'd really like to do so. Of course I would reimburse you what you paid for it."

"Well, Clara was a distant cousin of mine and I must say this is a bit disappointing as I'd rather like to keep it myself."

"Yes, I thought that there must be some family connection what with your name being Momford and I can quite see your position."

"Well, I'm away at the moment in France so there's not much I can do for you here and now…"

"Oh, I see. Look, I don't want to be unreasonable about this and I entirely understand that you want to keep the book. Perhaps as an alternative you'd consider lending it to me for a period?"

"Yes of course. That sounds a very happy compromise."

"Good, good. Perhaps you'd be so kind as to get in touch with me after you return to England, at your convenience of course, no hurry."

I agreed and after wishing me a nice holiday and giving me his landline number and email address, he rang off.

"What was all that about?" Charlotte asked.

"What a bloody cheek!" She said after I'd told her, "come on, let's go."

***

Inevitably, it took a little longer than anticipated but we found the villa eventually.

It was still pink with green shutters and looked very well cared for. The driveway widened into a large forecourt in front of the building on which were parked a Mercedes estate car with a French number plate and a Porsche with an English one.

The garden was certainly no jungle. From the road, craning our necks we could see a modern state-of-the-art infinity swimming pool with sun loungers scattered around it, all shielded by luxuriant sub-tropical vegetation. Beyond lay a well-kept lawn culminating in a row of tall cypress trees and, visible between them jutting out into the sea and enclosing a small cove, a rocky promontory on which stood a magnificent, gazebo of wrought-iron in an art nouveau design.

I was in the process of taking photos with my mobile when a man emerged from the house, walking purposely towards us down the driveway.

"Good morning," he said in excellent English as he reached the gate. Presumably, he thought we looked English or perhaps he was himself English – difficult to say.

"Good morning," Charlotte and I replied more or less in unison.

"I don't wish to appear disobliging," he continued in a distinctly upper-crust English accent. "But this is a private home you know. We value our privacy here and would prefer it if you would kindly desist from peering in at us and taking photographs."

"Oh, I'm sorry," I said. "We had no wish to be intrusive but you see I have a particular interest in this house as it used to belong to my cousin Clara Momford."

"Really?! Oh well… Of course now I understand" he said in an altogether friendlier tone of voice. "Please feel free to take as many photos as you wish."

"Thank you. I must say the villa still looks very much as Clara describes it in her book, though now it's plainly in much better condition than it was when she first saw it."

"Oh, so you have a copy of the book, do you? Passed down through your family, no doubt."

"Well, actually no. I'd no idea that she'd written a book. Indeed, I knew very little about Clara herself. Quite by chance,

I found a copy in a local charity book shop and in perfect condition too."

"Good heavens! That was very lucky. It must be long out of print and quite rare now. I wonder why someone wanted to dispose of it."

"Well, I had a call this morning from the previous owner whose wife had taken it to the local charity shop by mistake and he'd like it back. He told me that it had been stored away in the attic for years and he'd never read it."

"Did he, indeed? May I ask, what was the name of this person who phoned you, wanting to have the book returned?"

"Matthew Duncan. Do you know him?"

"No, but I know the name. There was a man called Duncan who lived in Monte Carlo who advised ex-pats on business and financial affairs between the wars and later during the fifties, including members of my own family."

"That's right! In fact I recall now Mr. Duncan referring to his grandfather as a business advisor to ex-pats on the Riviera, Clara included."

"Well that would seem to clinch it. Look, perhaps you'd like to come in and have a look round the villa since you're here? I'm Gerard Belcourt," he added, pronouncing 'Belcourt' in the English way though the name, I thought, could of course be French.

"Oh, yes please, we'd love to…that's most kind of you. I'm Geoff Momford and this is my wife Charlotte."

We were led into the house and shown into a large drawing room furnished with a mix of furniture from the twenties and thirties – a classic suite of art deco sofas and chairs, Tiffany-style dragonfly table lamps, a gorgeous art nouveau black-lacquered cocktail cabinet in a faux-oriental design and much more besides. There were a few contemporary pieces chosen with great taste to blend well with the older furniture.

"I believe that most of the furniture and pictures in this room and the dining room originally belonged to Clara."

Double doors decorated with marquetry in a distinctive floral pattern gave access to a magnificently elegant dining room furnished and decorated in the same style as the drawing room only more so.

"Just wonderful!" Exclaimed Charlotte in wide-eyed admiration.

"Superb!" I added.

"Let's go onto the terrace and have something to drink." Gerard invited us.

There was a lady already on the terrace basking on a sun lounger whom Gerard introduced as his wife Lucille.

"Marie!, Marie!" Gerard called out. A middle-aged woman in a white apron appeared almost instantly from nowhere.

"Marie - Quatre Kir Royals, s'il vous plait."

"Oui, Monsieur."

As we sipped our drinks on the sun terrace overlooking the garden, which was even more extensive than was evident from the road, I tried to imagine parties that Clara had hosted there – parties for the cream of society, the beautiful, the famous, and the 'bright young things'.

"Are you on holiday here, staying on the Cap?" asked our host.

"Actually we're staying in Villefranche with friends. They have a flat there."

"Oh, how nice! Is the flat in the old town?" Lucille asked. She spoke English well but with a marked French accent.

"Yes, almost opposite the Patisserie Giselle?"

"Oh, yes. I know where you mean."

***

We must have been there for some time, talking of this and that. It transpired that I'd been half right about Gerard. He was part English, part French and had been educated in England. Lucille was French and from these parts but she'd been educated at a private convent school in Paris and at university in London. I estimated that they must both have been in their fifties. Eventually, Charlotte nudged me, sensing that it was time for us to leave.

"Oh, about Clara's book," Gerard said, as we rose from our chairs.

"Yes?"

"I would be prepared to make you an offer for your copy. It's quite rare as I said before, a collector's item in fact. I would be robbing you if I were to offer you less than say £150 for it. Frankly, I don't think you owe any duty to Mr. Duncan to return it. What do you say?"

I saw Charlotte, who was standing directly behind Gerard, frantically gesticulating to get my attention and mouthing the word 'No'.

"Well," I replied. "It's a most generous offer but, in view of the family connection I would really prefer to keep it. Besides, I haven't yet finished reading it myself and I've offered to lend it to Mr. Duncan when I get home. I don't want to go back on my word."

"If you change your mind please let me know. Here's my card. The offer remains open."

***

"That was strange," Charlotte said as we made our way down the Rue Mirabeau towards the main road.

"What was?"

"The offer to buy Clara's book. I'm sure he must have a copy of his own in any case. Glad you didn't accept. I bet it's worth a lot more money than he offered you."

"Maybe."

"Tell you what," Charlotte said, changing the subject. "Why don't we visit the Rothschild Villa on the way back. I know we've been there several times, but it's so beautiful and I enjoy it more each time we go."

"Okay. Fine with me."

Villa Ephrussi, often referred to as the 'Rothschild villa' is located on a promontory near St Jean de Cap Ferrat. It was built in the early twentieth century for Baroness Béatrice de Rothschild as a seaside home. When she died in 1934 it passed under her Will to the Académie des Beaux Arts and opened to the public.

The villa always seemed to me like a giant pink wedding cake but nevertheless I found it an attractive and cheerful sort of building. It houses important collections of old master paintings, antique furniture and porcelain but is perhaps most famous for its lovely gardens, nine in all, each with a different theme: among them a French garden in a formal style with topiaries, a typical Japanese garden, a Spanish garden complete with fountain and shady courtyard, an exotic garden with enormous cacti and tropical plants, a remarkable garden decorated with Sevres porcelain and a superb Florentine garden with a grand stairway and Italian grotto.

Every time I visited the villa I always came away feeling up-lifted and this time was no exception – rather like listening to a well-loved piece of music of which one never tires however often it's played.

It was the middle of the afternoon by the time we returned to the flat, just time for a short siesta to take us up to 'Cocktail Hour'. John fancies himself on his ability to mix cocktails and I had to admit that the dry martinis he served that evening were as good as any I'd ever tasted, a fitting end to a day, one of those rare days when everything works out even better than planned.

Later that evening as I lay in bed, I read a little more of Clara's book in which it transpired that on the way back to Menton after the lunch party with the friends of the Benthams, she too had visited the Villa Ephrussi. It was of course still privately owned at that time. Baroness Rothschild was not there, how-ever, as she was generally only in residence during the winter months but the caretaker instantly recognized the Benthams as friends of the Baroness and invited them all in to explore the house and gardens. All this gave me the pleasing feeling of following in Cousin Clara's footsteps. Yes, it had indeed been a very good day I told myself – and I had not even given a moment's thought to the matter of Cloverton Hall and its fu-ture. More fool me…

6

I woke up early as usual and from its very beginning the day started badly and continued so.

With a deep sigh I hauled myself out of bed and in doing so trod on something. It turned out to be Clara's book. I must have fallen asleep reading it and it had slipped off the bed. I noticed that the binding had been slightly damaged in the fall and the back cover had come partially adrift. It probably didn't help that I'd trodden on it as well.

"Damn, damn, damn!" I muttered to myself.

"What, what, what?" Charlotte murmured before turning over and resuming her sleep.

After a quick shower I got dressed and clutching the book, made my way quietly to the terrace in accordance with my normal routine.

I examined the book again. The damage was not, I thought, irreparable. There was an antiquarian bookshop near my office in Birmingham and the chap there also provided a bookbinding service. He had re-bound and repaired one or two old books of mine and I felt sure that he'd be able to sort out Clara's book without too much difficulty or expense.

The bookmark had fallen out when the book dropped to the floor and it took a little while for me to find my place.

Eventually I was back on course and after a couple of pages, Clara went on to describe the rest of her holiday with the Benthams – during which nothing much of a great interest happened other than a visit to the casino in Monte Carlo.

On her return to England she found a letter from her mother awaiting her.

My Dearest Clara,

I was so happy to meet you in London and to get to know you a little and I hope perhaps you will now have a better opinion of your poor mother.

I fully understand that you regard Mr. And Mrs. Parfitt as your true parents, that you love them dearly and that they in turn love you as a daughter. This is only right, but please know that I also love you and that in all these years you have never been far my thoughts. I dare to hope that there will always be a small space in your heart reserved for me too.

My darling, I have become now a very wealthy woman, underserved as that may be. I have more money than I can conceivably want or need. I have accordingly arranged to transfer a certain sum to Charles's bank and have asked him to open an account with it in your name. I do hope this gift will, to some degree at least, make up for the way I brought you into this world only to give you away.

I hope too that we may continue to keep in touch and that one day we shall see each other again.

With every fond wish,

Your loving Mother, Grace

Well, well, well, I thought, how very kind of her. My second thought was of course to wonder how much. Perhaps five hundred pounds, I dared to hope but even a hundred would be more than generous.

The next day I telephoned Charles, eager to learn the amount involved.

To say that something causes one 'nearly to fall off one's chair' has become a cliché but the fact is that there was no 'nearly' about it. I did fall off my chair.

Mother had transferred a sum which when converted from dollars to sterling amounted to more than a quarter of a million pounds.

This was truly extraordinary! A quarter of a million pounds then, would equate to nearly ten million in today's money.

Having recovered and restored herself to an upright position, Clara expressed the first thought that entered her head:

My God! I can now buy and restore the Villa Mirabeau and have a colossal fortune left to live on. Louis was right! Fate had indeed smiled on me as he foretold it would, but with a much bigger and broader smile than I could possibly have imagined!

First of all she decided to contact Louis with the news and to ask for his help. He had told her that he lived in Paris but had insisted, rather mysteriously, that if she ever wanted to make contact with him she should do so via the head porter at the Negresco Hotel in Nice, where he usually took a suite for his frequent visits to the South of France.

She had some doubts that she would ever actually hear from Louis but a day later she received a telephone call from him.

He was delighted that she wished to buy the villa and had now had the means to do so. He recommended a man who could help her with the negotiations and ensuing formalities. His name was Frank Duncan. Well, I thought, that fitted well enough with what Matthew Duncan and Gerard Belcourt had told me.

As Clara writes:

"Frank Duncan", Louis informed me, "lives in Monte Carlo. He claims to be of noble Scottish ancestry and puts on rather grand airs, dropping casually into the conversation mention of castles, fishing lodges and shooting estates, though a lawyer friend of mine from Edinburgh swears that his grandfather was in fact a ghillie on the River Tay and his father was a Glasgow bookmaker. In any event Frank married a statuesque beauty called Josephine, the widow of a wealthy merchant of French Algerian descent whom he met apparently on a business trip to Algiers. They eventually settled in Monte Carlo where Josephine had relatives of some importance."

Whatever can be said about him, Louis went on "Frank is undeniably very good at fixing things. He knows the ropes and all the right people too. I suspect that he may not always be entirely scrupulous in his business dealings and it would not do to ask too many questions. However, he gets things done and I have no hesitation in recommending him to carry out negotiations on your behalf for the purchase of the villa. I'm in no doubt that he will secure it for you at a good price. Not only that he would, I'm sure, also arrange the necessary formalities with customary expedition and efficiency, saving you a great deal of trouble.

"Normally, he charges a healthy fee for his services and often takes a cut of any deal in which he is involved. However, he happens to owe me a big favour and I think I can persuade him in this case to provide his services free of charge. If you agree, I will contact him on your behalf and ask for his assistance."

I continued reading.

Clara had hastened to agree to Louis's suggestion and matters were put in hand.

After some to-ing and fro-ing, a deal was duly agreed and as Louis had prophesised, Frank indeed secured the villa for Clara at a very good price. Frank arranged for a notary to undertake the legal work and completion was fixed for a date a month or so later at the notary's office in Nice.

At this point in the narrative I heard voices, and put the book down. Before heading for the kitchen where no doubt breakfast was being prepared, I thought I had better check my phone for any messages. I found an email from my neighbour Donald Watson sent the night before:

Hi Geoff,

Further to our last conversation about the Cloverton Hall planning application, I'm pleased to report that there've been 15 objections so far lodged with the planners.

Well, that's the good news, but I had a rather troubling conversation with Mark Bridges who, as you know, is our local councillor. He told me that the Chief Planning Officer is apparently recommending acceptance of the application and that some members of the planning committee are in favour of the proposals and others are wavering.

I must say that I find all this all quite worrying and it makes it all the more imperative that we get as many objections in as we can. I've got a little informal committee of locals up and running, as promised, and we're trying to arrange a public meeting at the parish hall for Friday week, by which time I think you said you would be back home. We're distributing a flyer about the meeting round as many households in the village as possible and also copies to display at the pub, tea rooms, shops etc.

I have also drafted a form of letter to go to organizations like the National Trust, English Heritage, the Council for the Protection of Rural England and other conservation groups to seek their support in opposing planning approval. I attach a copy and should be grateful if you kindly would cast your expert PR eye over it and suggest any amendments.

In the meantime, I hope you both have a very good time during the rest of your holiday and look forward to seeing you on your return.

Regards Donald

I shared Donald's concerns. Until now I had been confident that planning permission would be refused. Charlotte, to whom I gave the latest news had also been sure. Now she was almost as concerned as I was.

"But why are these people apparently in favour of this awful proposal?"

"Well, the Council is always trying to promote new business in the district and to create employment. I imagine that must be the reason."

"But we don't need any of that, do we?"

"I quite agree with you, Charlotte. People are attracted to our village for its charm and peacefulness, the views, the nice country walks and so on and there's no problem with unemployment locally. I suppose some think that local traders, the food shops for example might benefit, though in my view, that would be misguided. I'm sure that if planning permission were granted the business would be managed by a specialist company, likely to be operating in other venues. If that was the case I suspect they would use a central ordering system with established national suppliers for everything that they needed. I doubt in any case the local shops would be big enough to cater for them."

"What about B&Bs and the pub which has a few rooms?"

"Well, the local B&Bs and the pub might attract overflow guests, I mean those for whom there's might not be room in the guest accommodation at the Hall. But this would be at the expense of losing custom from their regulars and others who come to enjoy the olde-world charm of the village and its beautiful countryside setting."

"Yes, yes, you're absolutely right Geoff – surely the councillors on the planning committee will see sense in the end and the application will be chucked out?"

"Well, let's hope so but not everyone will agree, especially if the Chief Planning Officer is recommending acceptance. I think we've got a battle on our hands."

As soon as I'd had some breakfast I checked through the draft letter which was attached to Donald's email.

Meticulous lawyer that he was, Donald had set out the facts and arguments very clearly but the draft was, I considered, a little too dry and legalistic. I felt that it needed to be a bit 'punchier' to encourage the sort of response we wanted. As soon as I could, I emailed my suggestions back to him, wishing him all the best with them and adding that I would be home in time for the proposed meeting.

***

The plan for that day was a trip to Antibes to visit the Musée Picasso and have lunch at one of John's favourite restaurants. John has many favourite restaurants. In fact it would probably be much easier to list those restaurants, if any, that were not his favourites, but he assured me that this particular restaurant was a favourite among favourites; that their Bouillabaisse was the best he had ever tasted; that the tarte Tropézienne, a favourite dish apparently of Brigitte Bardot, was 'epic' and that their wine list was 'quite without peer'.

Even in the face of such a glowing review Charlotte, who had heard all this sort of talk before, decided that she would prefer to opt out of the trip and stay at home. The previous night had been extremely hot and stuffy and unusually for her, she had not slept well. A relaxing day on the terrace with a good book would, she felt, do her more good.

So just the three of us, John, Anna and I, set off in John's car for our day out.

I had never before visited the Musée Picasso, housed in an amazing building formerly the Chateau Grimaldi where for a short period Picasso himself had actually lived. I suppose that I had never really appreciated the breadth of Picasso's art and I was particularly taken with the wonderful ceramics displayed in the museum. Altogether, it was a most rewarding experience.

If the day had got off to a flying start it began to go seriously downhill thereafter. First, John's memory failed him and the restaurant was not quite where he thought it was. We spent time wandering around the old town in the mid-day heat trying to find it, jostled by crowds of people thronging the narrow streets.

"What time did you book the table for?" I asked him, getting rather concerned.

"Oh, I didn't bother to book, but I'm sure it will be all right."

"What if the place is full?"

"Oh, it won't be. Don't worry."

Well when eventually we found it it wasn't full. It was closed.

After more traipsing round in the fierce heat (all restaurants by then full with long waiting times), we finally settled for a singularly unprepossessing brasserie in a back street with a view of what appeared to be a cycle repair shop.

There was no Bouillabaisse on the menu. The waiter had never heard of tarte Tropézienne and for our sweet course we had to settle for a very ordinary tarte Tatin. As Anna, who is always ready with a nice line in sarcasm, commented:

"I'm not sure that Miss Bardot would have entirely approved of this tarte Tatin, do you,? even if it had been a little less soggy."

Rather disconsolately we made our way back to the car, parked in the shade when we arrived but now in the full glare of the sun. To call it boiling barely did justice to the pizza-oven temperature inside the car and to cap it all, fate had chosen just this day for the air conditioning to pack it in.

It was a thoroughly irritable, weary, sweaty trio that finally returned to the flat in Villefranche.

Happily Charlotte had prepared a superb supper for us which cheered everyone up and John, to make amends for his failure to check that the restaurant was open, served up another bottle of his very special rosé. He had begun to rhapsodize yet again on its ultra-special qualities when he was mercifully interrupted by Charlotte.

"Oh, by the way," she said, "the plumber came this morning just after you left."

"Plumber?" John sounded a bit mystified. "I never called for any plumber."

"Well, he said he'd come to repair the leak in the bathroom. At least that's what I thought he said if I understood the French correctly."

"What leak? I don't know of any leak in the bathroom... Christ! I hope this wasn't a con, an excuse to gain entry to the flat. This bloke could've been a thief! We better check that nothing's been stolen."

Amid exclamations of alarm we all promptly left the table to scurry around checking such valuables as we had: jewellery, laptops, cameras, passports and anything that might be of worth. Nobody reported any loss. Everything seemed quite in order.

"Well, thank God for that!" John said, sighing with relief.

"Perhaps this plumber chap had simply got the wrong apartment,"Charlotte mused. "He didn't stay long, just muttered 'Excusez-moi de vous deranger' and left with his toolkit".

"Yes, you're probably right. That could well have been it," John agreed, happy to accept what seemed like a plausible explanation.

Supper resumed, our glasses were topped up with John's precious rosé and we thought no more about it.

7

After an enjoyable evening making up for what had been a day of mixed fortune, the peculiar mystery of the unwanted plumber quite forgotten, we all retired to our beds in a better frame of mind.

As usual I thought I would read a few more pages of Clara's book to help relax my mind for sleep.

It took some minutes before I realised something was amiss, something strange.

"But this is not my book!" I said out loud, sitting up in bed.

"What are you talking about?" Charlotte, who had just been about to drift off to sleep, asked yawning.

"This is not my book!" I repeated.

"What do you mean 'not your book'? Of course it's your book, the book by your cousin Clara you've been reading every day since we got here. I recognise the cover."

"It isn't, I tell you. I mean not *this* copy of the book. This one is in perfect condition."

"But your copy was in perfect condition. You told me so yourself. You're talking in riddles."

"No, my book *was* in perfect condition but it was damaged when it fell off the bed this morning. This copy isn't damaged at all."

"But this is extraordinary! Are you quite sure?"

"Absolutely. It must have been that plumber or whoever it was masquerading as a plumber. He must have substituted the books."

"But why on earth? Is the book you've got now any different from the other one?"

"No, not that I can see at least. It's a complete mystery."

I could see that Charlotte didn't really believe me. She clearly thought I was mistaken. The whole thing made no sense.

"Ah, well," she said. "Life is full of mysteries. I dropped my watch in the bathroom this morning and could have sworn the glass face was cracked but when I looked again there was no sign of any damage."

"Well, I tell you this is not my book."

***

The next day we all set off to visit the Camargue, a trip John had suggested when we'd met for dinner in London some months before to discuss the holiday.

Charlotte and Anna had both expressed a desire to see the wild white horses and flamingos that famously inhabit the marshy plains and wetlands of the region, while John wanted to see the Roman amphitheatre in Arles nearby and, of course, try out a restaurant which he said had had 'ecstatic reviews'.

The restaurant was part of a hotel and we stayed there for two nights.

What with the menu gourmand on each night with a different wine to accompany each of the six courses and Armagnacs to follow I felt much like Charles, Clara's father must have felt after the lavish lunch with his Uncle Eustace. I slept better than usual, however, and didn't manage to read very much more of Clara's book.

On the morning following our return to Villefranche, Charlotte, John and Anna decided to go into Nice to do some shopping. I had other ideas.

 "I've been thinking about the book switching mystery," I said. "I suspect this has got something to do with that fellow Belcourt at the villa. I'm going back there to ask a few questions."

Charlotte thought me quite mad.

"What are you going to say to the man, for heaven's sake – accuse him of theft? You'll get nowhere except to make yourself look foolish!"

Nevertheless, I took a bus to St Jean de Cap Ferrat and walked to the villa. I rang the intercom bell by the gate. After what seemed a long wait, a French voice answered which I recognised as Marie, the Belcourt's housekeeper who had produced the Kir Royals on our recent visit.

"Non. Je regrette mais Monsieur Belcourt n'est pas ici… ni Madame Belcourt."

I asked when they would be back but Marie informed me that they'd gone to an exhibition in Cannes and thought that they'd be gone all day.

Well that was that.

Irritated that I had wasted my time, I concluded that Charlotte was probably right. Even if Gerard had been there it was hardly likely that he would have admitted employing a thief to steal my book. All I had to look forward to was Charlotte saying 'I told you so' and calling me 'a bloody fool' – which I suppose I deserved.

The mystery, however, remained a mystery.

On returning to the flat I poured myself a beer from the fridge and repaired to the terrace with, I was still quite sure, was a different copy of Clara's book. Significantly, I thought, the bookmark was missing, but I found my place and began reading:

The date for completion of the purchase of the Villa Mirabeau finally approached. A few days before, I set forth to Nice with Margot, who had insisted on accompanying me. As the train travelled south through France, I became increasingly excited. Soon the villa would be mine and I had by then half decided…more than half decided… that I would make it my permanent home. It had been my dream when I first saw the villa but never thought that it would actually happen.

Charles had arranged for a banker's draft in French Francs in the vendor's favour for the required balance of purchase money for me to take to Nice, along with a further draft in favour of Mr. Duncan to reimburse him for the notary's fees and other accounts which he had agreed to settle on my behalf. The relevant formalities had been all been satisfied in readiness for completion, and all that remained to happen was the meeting at the notary's office when the legal sale document transferring the property into my name (now changed to Momford) would be signed, the notary would affix to it his notarial seal and the banker's draft would be handed over.

Louis would meet us in Nice. He had insisted on being there 'to hold my hand', as he put it though, as I half expected, it was other parts of my anatomy which he really had in mind … not that I minded.

He had arranged accommodation for us at an apartment in Nice owned by a Parisian friend of his. He would be staying there, too, instead of his usual suite at the Negresco. His friend would not be there and there were accordingly three bedrooms available, he said – enough for us all.

We arrived in Nice in the early evening on the day before the property completion meeting. Louis met us at the station and, after our luggage was deposited at the apartment, took us to a very smart restaurant for dinner.

The apartment, to which we returned quite late, was very charming and Louis had allocated to me quite the nicest room with a view overlooking the Vieux Port. I had only been in bed for a short while when Louis appeared.

"Was I quite comfortable?"

Yes, I was.

"Was there anything else he could do for me?"

Well, there he was in his exquisite silk dressing gown with the oriental dragon motif looking so desperately handsome, and there was I intoxicated by the whole business – not to mention an indecent quantity of wine and champagne.

Of course there was something he could do for me.

"Oh, yes, yes," I murmured, half-hoping that he wouldn't hear and half-hoping that he would.

"Oh, yes," I repeated, in a slightly louder voice, just in case.

The silk dressing gown gracefully cast aside, he slipped into bed with me. It was to be the beginning of a long on-off affair.

At breakfast the next morning I wondered if Margot had also enjoyed a nocturnal visitation but, if she had, she was not saying anything and neither was I.

Soon it was time to make our way to the notary's office about ten minutes' walk from the apartment.

The meeting was quite a formal affair and I was nervous in case something went wrong. I need not have been, however, as Frank Duncan who was also present had left nothing to chance and the notary conducted matters with brisk efficiency. Madame Hulbert, the vendor, was too old and frail to attend in person and was represented by her son, Gustave, to whom his mother had given the French version of a power of attorney enabling him to sign on her behalf.

After the meeting I offered to take Louis, Margot, Frank and Monsieur Hulbert out for lunch at the Negresco to celebrate my purchase of the villa. Monsieur Hulbert politely declined as he was returning almost immediately to Paris, and Frank Duncan also declined as he said he had other business to attend to.

So that left only Louis, Margot and me.

I was sorry that Frank Duncan had not joined us as I had wanted to repay him for all his efforts in securing the villa for me.

"Frank is not sociable, at least in the way that you, I and Margot are," Louis explained. "He has few real friends. Most of the people he knows are business acquaintances or people who might be of some use to him in advancing or protecting his interests. He rarely accepts invitations to parties. He prefers to hold court at a restaurant in Monte Carlo which he jointly owns with his brother-in-law, an expensive but rather vulgar establishment with enormous chandeliers, faux marble columns, throne-like chairs and plush red velvet cushioned banquettes. It is where he entertains those whom he wants to impress."

In fact, the lunch was the more enjoyable with just the three of us and the champagne of course went further. The celebrations continued on a luxuriously appointed yacht, moored in the marina, owned by an old friend of Louis: a wealthy and most hospitable Armenian gentleman. Finally, we returned to the apartment and all three of us tumbled into the same bed.

"That was quite the most wicked night I have ever spent," Margot said next morning. "It was nothing short of sheer debauchery."

"Fun, though, wasn't it?" I said.

"Delicious fun! But our parents must never know."

Margot's last point, about their parents never being allowed to know what their daughters were getting up to, raised an interesting question. Why? When it appeared Clara had gone to some lengths to conceal the identities of many of the people mentioned in the book. Was she not equally concerned to shield her own and Margot's identities, especially from their parents? The book was not finally revised and completed until July 1946 and not published until March 1947, by which time Clara's parents, both natural and adoptive, had passed away, as had Margot's.

Otherwise, neither Clara nor Margot seemed to have the remotest concern themselves for their own reputations or what people might think of them. Indeed, they seemed rather to revel in being outrageous. As Margot says in her preface Clara loved 'to shock', and indeed she was probably quite right in thinking that people rather enjoy being shocked while pretending to be outraged and offended.

Casting these thoughts aside, I continued reading.

"Louis's such a rogue, isn't he?" Margot said.

"Yes, but a very lovable one," I replied.

"So lovable that I think one of us will probably end by marrying him!" Margot said, rather pointedly.

Over breakfast Margot, in her customary forthright manner, asked Louis why he kept returning to Paris. Why, when he clearly seemed to prefer life in the South of France and spent so much time there, did he simply not move there permanently? Why, Clara had added for good measure, was it only possible to contact him when he was away in Paris through the head porter of the Negresco?

At first Louis's answers were evasive but, badgered by Margot and Clara, he finally admitted that he was in, fact, married. He and his wife resided at a mansion in the Rue de Monceau. All her friends lived in Paris and she had absolutely no intention of moving elsewhere.

Margot and I looked at each other, wide-eyed.

"But, my darlings," Louis protested, "I'm only married in Paris. I've never regarded my conjugal vows as extending beyond the Île de France."

Well, at least I suppose, we were spared an unseemly contest to be first to elicit from Louis a proposal of marriage.

Nevertheless, despite my later acquired reputation as a racy socialite, I do have some sense of morality and was not entirely comfortable to be having an affair with a married man. Louis assured me, however, that his wife also had a life of her own and 'got up to things' so that he didn't consider his behaviour, when away from Paris, a betrayal. It was best though, he said, "to keep these things a secret if only to avoid upsetting the servants." Hence the special means of contact.

Gasping slightly over the unexpected revelation of Louis's marital status, let alone his rather original view of the extent of his marital obligations, I read on for a little while.

Later that morning Clara, Margot and Louis visited the villa. Louis had arranged for an architect friend of his to meet them there, and a landscape designer whom the architect had recommended soon joined them. Provisional plans were agreed for the restoration of the villa and the garden, which would include a new wider terrace for summer parties.

A few days later, Clara and Margot returned to London.

Leonard and Helena Parfitt, Clara's adoptive parents, were aware of the very substantial gift of money which Clara had received from Grace, her natural mother in America, but it was only on a later weekend visit that she plucked up the courage to tell them that she had purchased a villa in France. That she intended to make it her home and that she had already given up her job in London.

It had been a difficult conversation and the Parfitts were understandably upset and concerned.

"But what on earth are you going to do down there?" My poor father asked.

"I shall entertain lots of interesting people and I shall write a book," I replied. "But, don't worry. I promise that I shall return to England regularly to see you and always, of course, for Christmas." It was a promise that I'm proud to say that I have always kept.

I put the book down and consulted my watch. It was about the time that John and I went to the local bar for our customary early evening drink. There was still no sign of him, Anna and Charlotte. No doubt they had decided to stay on a little in Nice and go for a drink at one of the many bars near the Vieux Port, so I decided that I might as well go off for a drink in any event, John or no John.

Arriving at the bar, I made myself comfortable on the outdoor terrace and waited to be served.

Just then, I noticed a pretty young lady at the other end of the terrace who smiled and fluttered her eyelashes as she looked in my direction. It's always encouraging for a man in middle age when a pretty girl pays him some attention, though likely as not she was looking at someone else altogether. Still, I thought, I can always dream; and I was still dreaming when the waiter came to take my order.

It was a gorgeous evening, the best time of day: sunny and warm and without the fierce heat of mid-afternoon. I took my time over my Kir before walking back to the apartment, taking a different more circuitous route along the little streets, up steps and through the narrow alleyways of the charming old town.

I had got about half way up the stairs of the apartment when Madame Flambert, who lived immediately below John and Anna, appeared on the landing. She keeps an eye on their apartment when no-one's there and has a key. Always a friendly and helpful soul, Charlotte and I are well-known to her as regular visitors.

"Ah, Monsieur, le plombier est arrivé. Je lui ai donné la clef."

"What?! The plumber again! Oh, my God!" I knew at once that whoever it had come was up to no good. John would have told me if a plumber was expected and asked me to stay in for him. This was surely a re-run of the book-switching incident. This was a thief, but what did he want this time?

Leaving a bemused Madame Flambert staring after me in incomprehension, I ran up the remaining flight of stairs and I had just reached the top when a short, thick-set man came charging out of the apartment. He cannoned into me, brushing me aside as he rushed on down. Turning round and trying but failing to clutch the banister rail I lost my balance and fell headlong down the stairs landing in a heap at the feet of poor Madame Flambert.

After much clucking like a startled hen in a mix of French and her Provençal patois, Madame Flambert fetched a pillow for my head and, hardly necessary, a blanket to cover my sprawling body.

Fortunately, fifteen minutes or so later John, Anna and Charlotte finally returned. John and Charlotte between them managed to help me to my feet and slowly up the stairs to the flat where, comfortably seated at last, I explained what had happened.

"How do you feel now?" Charlotte asked.

"A bit sore, but I don't think there are any broken bones."

But I was badly bruised; my left elbow and knee were rather painful and I think I'd sprained my wrist.

"This is all quite incredible," John said. "What on earth is going on? Better see if anything's been taken."

Unlike the previous occasion, this time the thief had left a bit of a mess with drawers and cupboards opened and their contents spilled over the floor. However, nothing seemed to be missing.

"And," said Charlotte, "he left his toolkit behind. I've just found it in the kitchen."

Like last time, it was all a bit of a mystery. Madame Flambert been about to go shopping and as she was leaving her apartment heard noises on the landing above. Being naturally nosy she had gone up to take a look. The thief was trying to break into the apartment when he heard Madame Flambert approaching. She asked what he was doing there and he said that he was a plumber who'd come to mend a leak in the bathroom. As there was no-one at home she had lent him the key.

This was hardly the relaxing French holiday to which I had looked forward – first, the email from Donald Watson with the worrying news of the Cloverton Hall planning application; then, unless I had imagined it, the peculiar theft of my copy of Clara's book and its replacement with another one; and now all this.

John poured me a large glass of Armagnac and Charlotte insisted that I take an early night.

9

Over the remaining period of our holiday I suffered from a recurring nightmare in which I kept falling downstairs – falling, falling, falling.

Though not wanting to admit it, I remained shaken by my recent experience and was happy to stay quietly on my own. I took the occasional walk around the town and along the sea-front, and paid a visit to the Chapelle St Pierre to view its amazing interior decoration by Jean Cocteau – balm for the soul.

Otherwise, apart from a few meals in restaurants nearby I was content to spend a peaceful time on the terrace of the apartment, taking turns to admire the lovely view, sleep a little and read more of Clara's book with which I made good progress.

***

Clara describes several further visits to the villa following her purchase, to observe progress with the works. On most occasions Louis came down from Paris to meet her and their affair continued. In the early stages they stayed in Nice until the works had progressed far enough for it to be possible to stay at the villa itself.

On one occasion, before travelling south, she stayed a few days in Paris at a magnificent apartment in the Rue Balzac with friends of Louis – broad-minded friends as Louis stayed there too, even though he lived not far away and, of course, he and Clara slept together.

> "And I thought the duty of fidelity to your dear wife applied at least in Paris, even if not elsewhere. Is that not so then?" I asked Louis, teasingly.

> "Ah, but only when my wife's in residence." He said. "At present, she's away in Normandy visiting her sister."

> "How very convenient for you!" I said with more than a hint of sarcasm.

> "For us, my dear, for us!" He replied, putting me in my place I suppose, with every justification.

It was not until April of the following year, 1923, that Clara moved permanently into the villa. A month later, she hosted her first party there. The refurbishment works were complete – including the new terrace specially designed for entertaining – and the garden re-landscaped. Organizing the party was a team effort between Clara, Louis and Margot, with Louis and

Margot providing the guest list and Clara supplying her natural charm and everything else.

> Louis seemed to know all sorts of people along the length and breadth of the Côte d'Azur, men, women, old and young, French, English and all sorts. He drew up for me a list of people to whom he thought it would be good to extend an invitation.
>
> Margot and her parents were spending more and more time at their villa in Menton, and she seemed to know most of the local ex-pats as well as French neighbours. Margot, whose regular company in France was as welcome as it was unexpected, also provided names of people to invite.
>
> I flatter myself that I have a natural talent not only as a party giver but as a party guest. At least, in all my time at Villa Mirabeau, I seemed to receive as many invitations as I myself issued. I have always been a sociable sort of person and Louis's and Margot's friends soon became mine too.

At any rate, Clara had gone to considerable expense and trouble to ensure the success of her first party and so it was, as she describes:

> I was nervous as the hour approached until the first guest arrived. Soon the party came to life: men in evening dress, elegant ladies in cocktail frocks shimmering with sequins, 'bright young things' in their flapper dresses, smart waiters busily circulating with canapés and refilling glasses with pink champagne, a jazz quintet playing numbers made famous by the Hot Club de France. It was all quite thrilling and I felt proud of myself.
>
> "Wonderful party, darling," Margot said after the last of the guests departed, "it really couldn't have gone any better."
>
> And I think, despite swaying back and forth like a drunken matelot, she truly meant it. Some people have referred to me as a socialite, whether meant as a compliment or otherwise. If true, then it all began that evening, but I have to recognise that my success, if success it be, would not have been possible without the support of Louis and Margot.

This was to be the first of many such parties, glittering occasions which showcased Clara's skills as a hostess, her beautiful villa, its lovely garden and indeed Clara herself who, to judge by the few pages of photographs in the book, had grown to be as beautiful a young woman like her mother had been.

She gained new friends. First through Margot and Louis and many more as she rapidly established an enviable reputation as a brilliant party giver. Not only beautiful but witty, intelligent and amusing company, she soon found herself much in demand. Anybody who was anybody, as she records without undue modesty, craved an invitation to the Villa Mirabeau and she herself was invited to all the best parties thrown by the rich and famous, from St Tropez in the west to San Remo in the east across the border in Italy.

Margot Bentham refers in her preface to 'scandalous goings-on' at the villa of which Clara's narrative provides ample evidence.

> Squeaks and squeals from the gazebo at the bottom of the garden could be heard, to my amusement, even above the playing of the band.

Louis, on his frequent visits, was able to attend many of her parties. At one such event he had asked her if he could invite some friends from his tennis club in Paris.

> About five young gentlemen duly arrived for the party but without wives or lady friends.
>
> "But where are they staying?" I asked. "I've no room for them here."
>
> 'Oh, don't worry. They are all going to stay on Petros's yacht.'
>
> Petros was Louis's wealthy Armenian friend on whose yacht Margot and I had once been guests.
>
> "Large enough for all that lot?"
>
> "But of course, Petros's yacht, as I'm sure you must remember, is the size of a small cruise liner."
>
> "Well, if you say so."

"Oh, and I hope you don't mind, but I've asked a few young ladies to come along so that they have some female company and won't feel left out of things."

"Well, you should have told me first…Who are these ladies?"

"Look…they've just arrived," he said, pointing towards the other end of the terrace.

Sure enough. There were a gaggle of over-made up, rather cheaply dressed young women. What, I worried, would the rest of my more sophisticated guests be thinking?!

"Yes, but who are they? Where did you dredge them up?" I asked, irritated to say the least.

"Oh, they're singing in the chorus in one of those Verdi operas currently running in Monte Carlo."

"They look more like cheap tarts to me, the sort who try to pick up wealthy-looking men coming out of the casino," I replied.

"Now, now, Clara. Don't be so beastly. They're nice girls and very talented, too."

At this point, more guests arrived to whom I had to attend. The party got under way and I did my best to forget about Louis's wretched girls.

A short while later I happened to notice Louis talking to someone near the swimming pool. It took me a moment or two before I recognised quite who he was. He was an egregious porky little man to whom I was once introduced at a bar in Nice. I had found out later that he was commonly known as Monsieur Fifty-fifty – a pimp who specialised in providing 'loose women' for naughty late-night parties at exclusive villas or on yachts in the marina.

It struck me immediately that I'd obviously been right all along about those girls… They may once have been chorus girls but not the sort that appear at the opera, and now they were, without any doubt, protégées of Monsieur Fifty-fifty, cheap tarts every one of them.

Furious, I strode across the lawn intending to give Louis a piece of my mind – a big, colourful piece of it too – but by the time I reached the spot both he and Monsieur Fifty-fifty had disappeared.

On the way back to the terrace I noticed one of Louis's Tennis club friends whom he'd invited to the party. He was on his own and I wondered where all the others were and indeed where were those girls.

"Vos amis, ou sont-ils?" I asked him.

"They have all gone with that man Petros to his yacht with the girls, Louis also," he replied in English.

"I see, but why did you not go with them?"

"There were not enough girls. One of them had gone off with another man. I didn't want to go on my own."

"Really? Well, what do you plan to do, I mean where are you going to stay tonight?"

"Louis said I could stay in his suite at the Negresco. He will be staying himself on the yacht tonight. He told me he'd fix it with the hotel."

"Did he indeed?! Well, that will be quite unnecessary. You can stay here at the villa."

"Oh, merci Madame…thank you, thank you."

"Ce n'est rien," I said, looking the young man up and down. He was a fine, tall, strapping man. You'll do very well, I thought.

I discovered later that his father was a high-ranking civil servant at the French Ministry of Finance. He was much too good for one of Monsieur Fifty-fifty's tarts.

"What's your name, by the way?"

"Je m'appelle Marcel."

"Well, Marcel, there's just one problem. All the spare rooms are occupied tonight, so you'll have to share with me. I hope you don't mind."

He didn't mind…

I don't think I've ever spent a more energetic night in my life…except possibly with Count Zoltan of whom more later. It took me a day to recover, but it was quite wonderful. Louis was very miffed when he got to hear of it, which pleased me enormously.

Marcel would not be the last fit young man to be seduced at one of Clara's parties – there were more virile French tennis players, energetic English cricketers, and dashing Italian racing drivers.

There was mention too of a memorably exotic, highly perfumed, young gentleman of Egyptian origin who claimed to be an Olympic athlete and a Cambridge rowing blue. Clara, writes:

This was all nonsense, of course – just hot air and stripey blazer. Ahmed was an outrageous poseur, but he had bags of charm and a novel repertoire of bedroom antics.

It seems there was hot competition between Clara and Margot.

If Louis was not in attendance and sometimes even if he was, Margot and I liked to compete for the attention of any handsome, unattached young man at the party. I suppose that this is how I acquired my reputation for being a bit of a femme fatale. What rubbish! It was all just fun, great fun. In any event, these games didn't necessarily always end up in tempestuous nights of passion, though some did. It was enough for the winner to lure a young chap to the gazebo for a canoodle. There was always much canoodling in the gazebo.

It might have become rather tedious had the rest of the book been entirely taken up with descriptions of parties, but it wasn't.

In any case, not all of Clara's parties were like her first one: exotic, no expense-spared affairs with limitless champagne a band, fireworks and all the trappings. There were other less grand occasions – informal, often wild – for local artists, writers, musicians and other Bohemian types at which occurred:

quite outrageous things, which I cannot bring myself to describe.

There were smaller cocktail parties for special friends and discrete dinner parties, too, some of which were less frivolous events with occasionally more serious conversations about politics, philosophy, art, music, opera and such like.

****

With so many parties of whatever nature to organise and with her book to write, Clara decided to employ a secretary. Frederick Latham was his name.

It was Margot who introduced me to Frederick. When I first met him, he was eking out a living in Nice as a translator but he had also been retained for a time by Sir Henry Bentham to proof-read his memoirs. By all accounts his had been a sad life. A gammy leg clearly caused him constant pain and had ruled him out of war service. Instead during the war years he had taught English at a preparatory school in Leicestershire.

At the school he had fallen in love with and married a young woman who worked in the school office. She had tragically died in the influenza epidemic just after the war ended. Not only that, the school had closed down shortly afterwards due to financial difficulties and he lost his job. He managed, however, through the recommendation of a friend to obtain a position as a private tutor to the daughter of a wealthy Italian family in Turin. He was paid a small salary and provided with accommodation and meals at the family home. He had only been there for nine months when the girl's parents decided to send her to a finishing school in Switzerland and, once more, he found himself out of work.

He was plainly an intelligent, well-educated man. I felt sorry for him but I also thought I could make use of him. I had just started to write this book and it occurred to me that it would be a good idea to have someone like Frederick to help me with it, correcting, editing and typing up the manuscript as I progressed with it. Also, I felt I could use the services of a secretary to assist with organizing my parties, dealing with correspondence and such like.

There was a small annexe to the villa which I believe had been constructed some twenty years ago for the occupation of a housekeeper. It consisted of a bed sitting room, a bathroom and a tiny kitchen. I offered this accommodation to Frederick together with what I judged to be a fair salary on terms that he would serve as my secretary, editor, proof reader and general factotum. He readily accepted the position. Indeed, he appeared overwhelmed with gratitude and I thought he served me very well.

10

It was not only her parties, it was, above all, Clara's interest in people, her descriptions of them and their stories that animated her narrative.

It was Louis who suggested that I invite Julie to a party. He had met her by chance while stopping off for a casual drink in the bar at the Majestic in Cannes.

She was a very striking woman who had been left a great deal of money by a wealthy shipping magnate, now deceased, whose mistress, Louis assumed, she must have been. She was always beautifully dressed in the latest Paris fashions and appeared to be a lady of some sophistication, but when she opened her mouth out came a deep, vulgar, throaty chuckle. She had a repertoire of bawdy jokes which she told at the top of her voice, jokes which would have shocked a convention of costermongers.

On other occasions she put on airs and graces as if she were a countess, and sometimes, she would suddenly switch from one to the other, catching people off guard – a trifle disconcerting to those who'd never met her.

I could forgive her anything because she had such style.

Julie indeed was a frequent guest at Clara's parties.

Parties can be very dull affairs. They need someone like Julie to ginger things up. I loved to see how people reacted to her. Of course, some were offended, though most, I think, were amused in spite of themselves. In any event, nobody has ever flounced off or declined another invitation or, indeed, failed thereafter to invite me to any of their parties. I only draw the line at cheaply dressed, over-painted little trollops, as I constantly remind Louis in case he should ever dream of inflicting such creatures on me again.

Men, of course, flocked round Julie like wasps round a crêpes Suzette. When Julie was around neither Margot nor I received the same attention, but I thought it worth the sacrifice as she always made things go with a swing.

I rather think that Louis, the little swine, took Julie back to his suite at the Negresco after one of my parties, but he never admitted it.

Louis was undeniably good at finding out things about people in whom he was interested. Beguiled perhaps by his natural charm and 'sympathique' manner, women in particular confided in him, revealing secrets about themselves that they would not normally dream of doing; and Julie was no exception.

According to Louis, Julie came from humble origins in the north of France. Her mother was a dressmaker but had been in service when she was young as a housemaid at a grand house near Rheims. Julie never knew her father but, though her mother never admitted it, she believed that he was in fact the master of the house where she was employed, a country gentleman of an old aristocratic family.

Her mother was apparently an excellent mimic and Julie must have taken after her which may explain that, like a good actress, she could play the part of a washerwoman or a duchess with equal facility.

Then quite suddenly she disappeared from the scene. Rumours abounded. She'd been seen, so people said, in Paris, Rome, Venice, London and even Los Angeles, but she never appeared again at the Villa Mirabeau. Wherever she was, she was an indomitable character and I wished her the best.

11

At John's suggestion, John, Anna and Charlotte had decided one morning to take a trip to a vineyard near Bandol. I declined to accompany them being happy as ever to spend the day on the terrace with Clara's book, a glass or two of wine, and the lovely view.

It was on this occasion that I read the rather disturbing story of Jack Costa.

There was invariably a gate-crasher or two at Clara's parties, or someone that Louis or Margot had invited without asking for her prior consent.

Jack Costa was quite definitely a gate-crasher and not even one of those invited on the sly by Louis or Margot. How he knew about the party I have no idea. He just turned up and behaved as if he was an old friend and a regular guest, though I couldn't recall ever having seen him before.

My usual way approach with gate-crashers is quite tactful – it has to be in case Margot or Louis had taken it upon themselves to invite them without my knowledge.

"Good evening," I would say, in a friendly but firm manner, "I wonder, by chance, whether you've come to the wrong party by mistake. I'm Clara Momford and this is my home, Villa Mirabeau. Perhaps you'd like to check the address on your invitation." I was about to proceed in this way, but Costa was surrounded with guests, one of whom, Dora, a wealthy English widow and neighbour of the Benthams in Menton, tugged at my sleeve.

"How thoughtful of you, Clara dear, to have invited Jack Costa to come to your party this evening. He's so much sought after, you know. Everyone wants to meet him."

"Really?" I said.

Before she mentioned it, I had not even known the man's name.

"Oh yes. He's a financial genius and he's helped so many people to increase their income. In fact, he's kindly coming over to see me next Friday to review my financial position."

"Surely, Dora, your financial position is more than secure. Your dear husband must have left you very well provided for."

"Yes, but one can always do with a little extra, don't you think?'

Somewhat bemused, and a little irritated, I decided not to intervene. Asking Costa to leave, however politely it was done, would upset silly old Dora and likely as not a host of my other guests.

To my annoyance, Costa had disrupted my party, turning it effectively into two separate parties: one of guests behaving as they normally would, chatting, laughing and drinking; the other clustered round Costa in ever-increasing numbers, hanging on his every word and quite oblivious to anything or anybody else. Each time I passed by I could hear the damned fellow holding forth and in deference to those making up his audience, first in English in a marked American accent then repeating himself in French and sometimes breaking into voluble Italian.

Without deigning to stop and listen properly I nevertheless caught a few random words and phrases:

….Shares in South African diamond mining company, Bulgarian steel-manufacturing combines, jute production in Moldova, South American railway shares, always selecting great opportunities for the fund to invest your money in, phenomenal growth potential, way above average income, highly regarded, reliable, great, great…

Thankfully after about an hour he left, thanking me profusely for 'a wonderful party'.

The evening never quite recovered its swing.

Clara asked Margot but she had never heard of Costa before.

Louis, who had been to London for a reunion party with university friends, arrived the next day and Clara asked if he knew anything about him.

Louis had no specific knowledge, though he said that he remembered meeting him briefly at a party in Antibes. He promised to contact Frank Duncan, the great local fixer and business advisor and a man who always seemed to know what was going on and who was who.

And indeed Frank was most informative. Clara records the facts passed on to her via Louis:

Costa had made his first appearance about eighteen months or so before when he had hosted a party at the Carlton Hotel in Cannes to introduce himself as the manager of an investment fund called Premier Riviera Investments.

Since then he had approached wealthy residents up and down the coast and persuaded them to invest often quite large sums in this fund. From the glossy prospectus Costa produced, the fund seemed to be both substantial and well-established with a well-spread portfolio of investments in profitable businesses and lucrative ventures world-wide. Very high returns were promised and, indeed, investors reported that the initial dividend income received and the quarterly capital valuations more than matched their expectations. Word got around and it was no wonder that Costa had little difficulty in securing a flood of keen new investors.

Frank, however, had reservations about him and his fund. He had advised friends and colleagues to steer clear of Costa until he had researched matters further.

Some days later Louis arrived at the villa with more news about Costa. Frank Duncan, with his customary diligence involving much cabling of friendly contacts in New York, Chicago, London and elsewhere, had finally got the full picture.

"It was good of Frank to go to so much trouble," I said.

"Oh, he really enjoyed it." Louis replied. "Frank likes nothing better than finding out things about people. 'Information is power!' he always says."

Essentially, to paraphrase Clara's narrative based on the information Duncan had managed to glean, Costa was a conman, a swindler.

The fund, Premier Riviera Investments, was operated by a shell company of which Costa was the sole director and shareholder. The fund in fact had no assets whatever, let alone investments in profitable businesses or lucrative ventures.

It seemed that Costa conducted his fraudulent business in a similar sort of manner to a 'Ponzi scheme', named after the infamous Italian fraudster Charles Ponzi, although Clara doesn't specifically mention Ponzi by name in her book.

Ponzi operated his scheme in America and Canada in the 1920s, at about the same as Costa, and became famous as a result of the very large sums involved in the swindle. Costa, also an American of Italian extraction, like Ponzi began his activities in America – albeit on a somewhat smaller scale.

The scheme was based on the 'robbing Peter to pay Paul' principle. Costa, known then as Jack Bruno, had never established an investment fund with any of the money entrusted to him by his clients. Instead, he pocketed most of it for himself, relying on funds received from subsequent investors to pay expected dividends. Then he would repeat the trick time after time. The quarterly capital valuations which he provided to each investor were simply fictitious but cleverly put together, in line with the bogus prospectus, so as to appear plausible.

For as long as there was constant stream of new investors there was a good chance that the fraud would go undetected. Once the stream dried up, or there was a significant demand from clients to cash in their investments, the whole thing would begin to unravel, as there would soon be no money left.

Bruno (Costa) managed to run the scheme for over three years in America, starting in New York before moving on to Chicago. Investment then began to slow up amid growing suspicions that the 'investment fund' was not all that it seemed. At this point, Bruno (Costa) disappeared before the authorities could catch up with him – unlike Charles Ponzi who was not so lucky and ended up in prison.

Bruno (Costa) surfaced some six months later in London where he embarked on a similar scheme. Here, the bogus fund was called 'The Anglo-American Enterprise Investment Fund'; he called himself Jack Lombard. He got away with it for nearly two years and, with the police actually on their way to arrest him at the swanky office in Mayfair, which he rented, he disappeared … only to emerge again as Jack Costa some months later in the South of France.

Hastily, I telephoned my silly old friend Dora and advised her on no account to invest any money with Jack Costa if she had not already done so. She told me that Costa had not turned up for his appointment with her.

Yet again Costa had managed to disappear in the nick of time.

However, some long while later the subject of Costa came up again. Louis had just returned to Cap Ferrat from Paris and he produced a cutting from a Paris newspaper. A man, it was reported, had fallen to his death from the third-floor balcony of a building in the Boulevard Raspail. He was described as 'the manager of an investment fund'.

A picture of the deceased appeared in the paper to accompany the article and there was absolutely no doubt at all that it was our old friend Jack Costa, though, of course, by then going under a different name.

"Did he fall or was he perhaps pushed by one of the many investors he cheated?!" I said.

"Perhaps he was pushed," Louis replied. "I wouldn't be at all surprised."

12

In many ways life on the Côte D'Azur could seem detached from what was happening in the rest of the world but sometimes world events would rudely intrude and force their way into Clara's narrative.

The years rolled on and the next chapter brought us to 1926 – the year of the General Strike in Britain.

I received a letter from Margot in the morning post.

She had returned to London with her parents for a short stay to see friends and relatives. I was both interested and amused by what she had to say:

Dearest Clara,

Have you read about the general strike here in England?

Workers everywhere refuse to turn up for work out of sympathy with the coal miners. Have you ever heard of such a thing?!

Many people are volunteering to do the jobs which need to be done to keep the country going. An old boyfriend of mine has volunteered to be a train driver, would you believe?!

As I've never driven anything in my life, I have offered to become a bus conductress, but dear Father vetoed the idea – not because he thought such an occupation was beneath me, but because, as he put it, my mathematical ability, or rather lack of it, simply wouldn't be up to the task and I'd give everyone the wrong change. Sadly, I think he is probably right so I shall have to think of something else.

We are all returning to Menton at the beginning of next month.

Fondest love,

Margot

The General Strike was soon forgotten and life at the villa continued in the same fashion for the next few years: more parties, more eccentric people and more scandalous behaviour.

Margot, even more than Clara, had a long succession of boyfriends, flames that flickered brightly but in the usual course of events quickly burnt out.

The boyfriends were of two types:

Those suitable to be introduced to her parents…boring,

Or those quite unsuitable…exciting!

One particular old flame, who burnt brighter than most and stood out from the crowd, was a man called Gino, an Italian and a handsome one too…at least for those who find the slick, devil-may-care look appealing.

Gino quite definitely fell into the latter 'quite unsuitable' category. He worked part-time as an entertainer in hotel and restaurant bars along the French and Italian rivieras between San Remo and Cannes, playing the piano and crooning popular songs. But this was only a base from which to practise his real profession. From Clara's description, he was the very embodiment of a lounge lizard, a gigolo adept at seducing older women, especially rich ones, who would pay for his services as an escort and, no doubt, services of a more intimate nature.

Plainly he liked to ape current American fashion both in the way he dressed and the way he spoke English – a classic drawl tempered by Italian charm. He wore correspondents' shoes, of course…but it was not only the shoes; he had a correspondent look in his eye and a correspondent smile on his face, not to mention hands which wandered in a most correspondent manner.

If the seduction of older women was for business, the seduction of younger women was for pleasure, and he was clearly attracted to Margot. Though hardly a young girl, Margot was, at thirty-three years of age, a good deal younger than most of his older quarries. Having chatted her up in the bar at the Hotel de Paris in Monte Carlo, he had taken her for a drive along the Grande Corniche.

After a short while, he pulled over into a layby, a most romantic location with a 'vue panoramique' of the coast and the Alpes Maritimes. Having admired the 'vue' for a moment or two, Margot was lured to the backseat of his motor car, where quite disgraceful but very pleasurable and exciting things had apparently taken place.

Margot brought Gino along with her to one of my parties. One or two of my guests, I suspect, unbeknown to their husbands, may have fallen victim to his undoubted charms and availed themselves of his more intimate services, episodes which no doubt they wished to keep very much to themselves. His presence was plainly an embarrassment and I banned her from ever bringing him again. She dropped him very soon afterwards and took up instead with Francois, an extremely handsome young French naval officer. Francois lasted rather longer than Gino but eventually she ditched him too.

I'm ashamed to admit, but only slightly ashamed, that I had the most wonderful time consoling poor Francois after Margot had given him the heave-ho.

Louis, who had been rather taking me for granted of late, was, I'm pleased to say, madly jealous.

One morning, I was just about to start on a new chapter of Clara's book when my phone pinged to indicate the arrival of a new text message. It was from Matthew Duncan:

Dear Mr. Momford,

Thought I'd let you know that I have managed to acquire a copy of Clara Momford's book in good condition on eBay for £22. Not bad, though you probably did better!

So, no need now to lend me your copy, but it would be nice to meet you some day.

Hope you're having a good holiday.

Regards,

Matthew Duncan

Well, I thought, odd that Gerard Belcourt should have offered to buy my copy for £150. Perhaps I should have accepted after all. Perhaps I should tell Charlotte, or perhaps not.

Dismissing the matter with a shrug, I continued to read:

About the same time as Margot's affair with Francois, I met an entertaining character at an art exhibition in Nice. He was well-known art dealer from London whom I shall call Tobias, not his real name. I chose Tobias for him because he reminded me of a cat of the same name who lived with a neighbour of the Benthams in Cheyne Walk.

Tobias, the cat, was a very precious animal, a Persian Longhair with a well-groomed coat of grey blue fur and dazzling blue eyes. He always seemed very pleased with himself to judge by the fact that he purred more than any cat I have ever known.

Tobias, the art dealer, was also a rather precious individual, an elegant figure of impeccable taste and exquisite manners, almost perhaps a shade too exquisite. Furthermore, he had a habit of extending the last word of every sentence he spoke with a sort of soft purr. He, too, seemed always very pleased with himself.

Tobias, the art dealer not the cat, was a frequent visitor to the Riviera as he had business connections with art dealers in Nice and Monte Carlo; I always invited him to my parties.

Louis once told me that a friend of his in the art business had heard a rumour that Tobias sometimes sold copies of works by well-known artists, passing them off as originals. The tale was that he employed the services of a brilliant forger, whose fakes would fool the experts and could only be detected by the most rigorous scientific examination.

So the story goes he sold these fakes to people of whom he disapproved – nouveau-riche types who buy art purely as an investment or a status symbol without any appreciation of their aesthetic value.

'Clara, my dear,' he told me after one dinner party, 'I do so love your parties. Your guests are invariably such charming and civilized people, so unlike the parvenus with whom one too often has to deal these days, the sort who believe that the purchase of a work of art or a Chippendale dining table will turn them overnight into gentlemen'.

There was never any specific evidence to support the rumour of Tobias's alleged dealings in forged art but he was without doubt an appalling snob. Perhaps I shouldn't have done, but I couldn't help but like him.

13

As I turned the pages the years rolled on and soon we had reached the autumn of 1929. Louis produced an English newspaper which he had bought in Nice; the lead story concerned the Wall Street crash the previous day, the 29 October 1929, the day that became known as Black Tuesday.

Bank failures had followed and panic set in. This was the beginning of the Great Depression. Initially it was the American economy that was most affected but as world trade plunged the effects spread across the globe.

Clara had worried about her mother but received a letter from her some weeks later to say that, whilst her investments had taken a knock, her financial position was secure; she had always had excellent professional advice. The New York stock market had in fact been falling since early September and her advisors had anticipated a crash – though perhaps not one quite so dramatic – and taken evasive action on her behalf. Many, however, had not been so lucky and some of her friends in the States faced extreme hardship, even ruin.

It took some time before France was as deeply affected, but not even the Côte d'Azur was impervious to the dire economic catastrophe that had engulfed so many other places. Complacent at first, many of Clara's friends and acquaintances suddenly found themselves with incomes much reduced and facing financial hardship. This especially applied to those who had already lost money in the Jack Costa investment swindle. Some even faced bankruptcy.

This was when, according to Clara, Frank Duncan came into his own. He along with a syndicate of wealthy associates was prepared to provide financial assistance by way of loan to those who were financially embarrassed provided they possessed hard assets: apartments, villas, yachts and so forth which they could offer as security – as indeed the majority were able to do. The terms were generous for an initial period with a low interest rate and delayed repayment of capital, but after this period had expired such terms became ever more onerous and default could result in foreclosure, even sequestration of assets. Frank of course charged a healthy commission on the setting up of each loan deal and he and his partners no doubt did very well.

Clara, as ever, took a pragmatic view:

> Louis thought all this was 'making money out of human misery, taking advantage of people when they were down'. Nevertheless, many were saved from the stigma of bankruptcy even though it may have cost them dear.

***

Clara, Louis and the Benthams, however, weathered the recession without too much financial pain and Clara was determined to keep her parties going if only:

> to cheer everyone up – I can't bear gloom and long faces.

If anything, the parties were even more lavish than before with dance troupes, entertainers and ever more spectacular firework displays, jazz bands, mountains of food and oceans of drink.

Life at Villa Mirabeau was not, however, all froth, frivolity and pink champagne. Clara had installed a grand piano in one of the villa's larger reception rooms called 'the Salon' which she now re-named 'the Music Room'. Louis was a gifted amateur pianist and Margot loved to sing.

Clara hosted regular musical evenings for selected friends and neighbours, and, on one occasion, Louis had managed to persuade a well-known concert pianist, whom he'd met in

Paris and who happened to be playing at a concert at the Théâtre National de Nice, to come and play for Clara and her guests one evening at the villa.

Clara was transported by the music.

> To hear Schubert's delightful impromptus played so beautifully and with such sensitivity under my own roof is a memory which I shall for ever cherish…

Dinner parties were often light-hearted affairs with salacious gossip and witty repartee at which Louis excelled; sometimes, as Clara had ever been keen to point out, they could also be occasions for more serious conversation. The best were blends of both and, fast-forwarding through the years to 1933, Clara gives a good example of one such dinner party.

> Louis, our resident raconteur, was at his amusing best. The star guest was, however, a professor of politics and philosophy from the Sorbonne who treated us to a most informative talk, delivered in faultless English, about the rise of fascism in Europe, its causes and the evils that would likely follow. This was timely, as a few days before, on the 30th January 1933, the German president Hindenburg had appointed Adolf Hitler as Chancellor, a big step towards the Nazis achieving their ultimate goal of total power, a goal which they would indeed achieve a few months later, in March, when the Reichstag, under duress, passed legislation enabling Hitler and his Nazi cabinet to rule by decree.

> There were many reasons for the rise of the Nazis in Germany and fascists elsewhere, as the professor argued, not least the economic depression. In Germany, this was amplified by the weakness of the Weimar Republic and the resentment felt by many Germans that they were hard done by and treated harshly in the aftermath of the last war, a resentment on which the Nazis were only too ready to play.

> "But," a guest interrupted, "has not Mussolini improved the state of things in Italy and restored Italian pride in their country and would not Hitler do the same for Germany? Was this not a good thing?"

> Admiration for Mussolini and Hitler is utterly misguided' the professor replied 'and the pride which Hitler seeks to promote is one based on fostering a belief in Aryan superiority in accordance with

Nazi racial ideology. A combination of German resentment and Nazi ambitions, I'm afraid, will lead to another war…"

"Oh, surely not," another guest cried out. 'Every sane person believes that the last war was 'the war to end all wars'. Another war in Europe is quite unthinkable!"

"I wish I could agree but I'm afraid the seeds of the next world conflict were sown in the last one. It only needs the right conditions for the seeds to germinate, and those conditions are rapidly converging."

"Unfortunately," Louis added for good measure. "Just because something is unthinkable doesn't mean it won't happen."

Of course, I thought, these issues may all be very familiar to us now. There have been reams written by historians, let alone television documentaries about the rise of fascism, Hitler and the Nazis and the causes of the Second World War but at the time of Clara's dinner party all of this would, I'm sure, have been both novel and controversial.

By all accounts there were many then who thought, if they thought about it all, that another war was inconceivable or, if the threat of war emerged, it could and would be avoided by compromise or appeasement.

Clara, however, as she makes clear in her book, took the professor's warnings more seriously and kept a weather eye on the way events were unfolding.

14

The last day of our holiday in France had arrived. The girls had decided to go together to Nice for a final day's shopping.

I thought I would like to pay one last visit to the Villa Mirabeau, if only just for the walk to Cap Ferrat. John, who had no wish to trail round the shops again with Anna and Charlotte, asked if he could accompany me.

I had only intended to look at the villa from outside and take another photo or two with my phone but as John was with me, I decided to be a little cheeky and ask for another view of the interior, the terrace and the lovely garden. After ringing the bell at the gate we waited; there was no response and we were about to turn away when a female voice crackled over the intercom which I recognised as Lucille, Gerard's wife.

"Oh, do please come in." She said, after I had explained who we were. I'm afraid that my husband, Gerard, is away at the moment. He had to go back to England for business. He'll be sorry to have missed you. I'd quite forgotten that Marie, our housekeeper, has the day off today and I'm sorry that I took so long to answer the bell."

"It's very kind of you to ask us in," I said. "I hope this is not too much of an imposition."

Lucille kindly gave us a guided tour of the villa, as Gerard had done on the previous occasion, before suggesting a drink on the terrace from where there was a good view of the whole garden including the famous gazebo which appeared to be in very good condition. I wondered idly if any canoodling still took place there. Probably not, but who knows?

John was quite as impressed as Charlotte and I had been on the first visit and I even more this time. As we walked away I must confess to feeling a little sad as it seemed unlikely that I would ever visit the villa again. It was not as if the owners were close friends; I could hardly keep turning up asking to be admitted. It may sound a bit fanciful but I had for want of a better expression, fallen in love with Villa Mirabeau just as Clara had all those years ago.

***

John and Anna were to remain in France for another few weeks. To mark the end of our stay and our gratitude for inviting us, Charlotte and I had asked them out for dinner that evening at a favourite restaurant in the town.

Before setting forth and while the girls were busy tarting themselves up after returning from their shopping outing in Nice, I had an hour or so to myself to read a little bit more of Clara's memoirs.

In early May of the same year, 1933, I received a letter from 'the Spanking Major'.

Roger, universally known as 'the Spanking Major', had joined the Army on leaving school. He had served on the general staff in the last war but a few years after the war ended had retired from the military to take over the running of the family engineering business on the death of his father. He was fortunate, however, to enjoy the assistance of a very competent manager which left him with plenty of spare time for travel.

He became known as the Spanking Major owing to his fondness for smacking ladies' bottoms.

The letter, couched in typical style, read:

My Dearest Clara,

At present, I'm staying for a few days in Paris with that young rascal Louis. If we have sobered up in time, we shall be travelling south together later this week by train. We should arrive in Nice by Friday evening, just in time for your next party to which Louis has invited me on your behalf. I do hope this is in order.

80

Incidentally, Louis tells me that you have been a very naughty girl and I shall of course be obliged to give you another good spanking.

Looking forward to seeing you,

With fondest good wishes,

Roger

I must say it was most gratifying, at the age of thirty-eight, to be referred to as 'a very naughty girl' and pleasing too that the Major, whom one might have thought would prefer younger bottoms, was still interested in my posterior. Mind you, I like to think mine was still shapely enough…and Margot's was a perfect peach.

As usual the major waited until the party was drawing to a close and the guests were leaving. Then he sidled up to me.

"Clara," he said, in a loud stage whisper, "it's time for your punishment."

Arm-in-arm we walked down the garden to the gazebo, where we found Margot canoodling with a swarthy young Frenchman.

"Bugger off, Margot," the major said. "It's your turn tomorrow," and the two of them set off up the garden, giggling as they went.

The gazebo stands on a short promontory adjacent to a little cove, right at the end of the garden, with a magnificent view over the bay. Inside it there is a suite of cane furniture comprising a small table and four chairs. The major turned one of the chairs around to face the view of the sea, sat down and beckoned me over.

"Standard procedure, Clara," he said. "You know the drill."

So I pulled up my dress and prostrated myself across his knee.

The spanking was more playfull than painful and there was a great deal of fondling between slaps.

"Clara," the major said after a short while, in a husky, urgent tone of voice. 'I must advise you that the sentry has just reported for duty."

"Yes," I replied. "I thought I could feel him stand to attention. Shall we go upstairs?"

And so we did, and I must say that Roger as always more than lived up to his name.

Though he must have been in his mid-sixties, the major cut a fine figure of a man with a magnificent handlebar moustache and a twinkle in his eye. I do so love a man with a twinkle in his eye and I've always been very fond the major.

***

I put the book down and looked again at the photo I'd taken on my phone that morning of the gazebo, a wondrous wrought iron structure, designed in an art nouveau style which reminded me of the entrance to the Metro station in the Rue des Abbesses in Paris. It was a nice photo but would have been even better, I thought, had it been taken on a moonlit night with the silhouetted figures of Margot canoodling with her Frenchman or the Spanking Major with Clara across his knee.

It had been a good final day, even if the rest of the holiday had been, to say the least of it, rather extraordinary.

15

We arrived at the airport in Nice next morning only to find that our flight home was delayed for two and a half hours 'for operational reasons'.

It was fortunate that I had Clara's book to read to help while away the time.

***

The narrative had become, I thought, a little uneven. Some of the ensuing years between 1933 and 1939 were dealt with in just a paragraph or two and some consumed a longer passage or a whole chapter. In many cases, this seemed to depend on a desire by Clara to write about a particular character or event that she considered to be of special interest.

One such event occurred at a cocktail party which Clara held in the spring of 1935.

Margot arrived accompanied by a man Clara didn't know and hadn't invited. He had disembarked at Genoa from a boat sailing from Port Said in Egypt and was on his way home to England. On the boat he had met a cousin of Margot's. They had become friendly and he had been prevailed upon to spend a few days with the Benthams in Menton before continuing his journey.

I must say I was a little annoyed with Margot, but she protested that she had spoken with Frederick, when I was out apparently, and he'd said that it would be perfectly all right to bring him.

At a glance, he looked about fiftyish, a tall, fit-looking fellow, with a tanned face and rugged features - not my type, though many would consider him handsome.

I suppose Margot must have introduced him to me, but I didn't catch his name.

Just after he and Margot had departed to return to the Bentham villa in Menton one of my guests, Martin Greaves, came over to speak to me.

Martin was another of Louis's friends, an Englishman who'd spent most of his life Africa but now worked for a yacht chartering company in Monaco. I'd always found him to be a jolly, easy-going type of character but when he came up to me he looked uncharacteristically serious.

"I've got something to tell you, Clara," he said.

"Go on then."

"It's about that chap whom Margot brought along this evening."

"What about him?"

"Well, he's not who Margot says he is."

"Really?"

"Yes. Margot introduced him to me as Lord Something or other …He shook me by the hand and asked me in a familiar way to call him

Hector. But I can assure you, Margot, the fellow's not a peer of the bloody realm nor is his name Hector. He's just plain Mister and plain John."

"But how do you know?" I asked.

"Well, I used to work for a shipping agent in Mombasa in Kenya and John worked for a ships' chandler business across the road from my office. I recognised him almost instantly, though he didn't recognise me. Later he got a job in the uplands, probably on one of those tea plantations. The man's a bloody imposter!"

A day or two later Margot dropped by. The wretched man had departed that morning on his way to England and I told her what Martin Greaves had said about him.

I knew that she'd be shocked and I'd planned a bit of gentle teasing to make her see the funny side of it, but I had underestimated her feelings. The fact was she was quite taken with him.

Poor Margot. As a young woman she had become engaged to a handsome Guards officer but it all fell through a month or so before the wedding was supposed to take place. Since then she had had many relationships over the years, none of which ever came to anything. Now approaching forty, like me, she had almost given up. Then along comes this man and something had clicked.

"There was something very special about him. Even though we'd just met I felt we were meant for one another," she said, the tears beginning to well up.

"Just as well, we know the truth, then…a lucky escape!" I said, in a vain attempt to cheer her up.

I asked Frederick to prepare a letter to the British Consul in Nice to report the matter for him to pass on to the Home Office or police in England or whomsoever might be appropriate. Martin had furnished the fellow's real full name and Margot reluctantly gave the lordly name and title by which she knew him and under which he masqueraded. She changed her mind, however, and insisted that the letter should not be despatched.

"John…though I shall always think of him as Hector…was such a kind and decent man. I can't really believe he was a fraud. I'm sure he would have been The One for me, title or no title. I cannot betray him."

Well, I thought to myself, I had found The One for me too but sadly Louis was unavailable – at least for holy matrimony.

What a bitch life can be!

***

A few more pages brought me to the Zoltan affair.

As she relates it, Clara first met Zoltan at La Reserve, a famous old hotel in nearby Beaulieu-Sur-Mer. An old friend from school days by the name of Vera Dalton, whom she was meeting for lunch at the hotel, had introduced them. Vera had recently lost her husband to a heart attack and was staying by herself at the hotel, as indeed was Zoltan. As Clara relates, based on what Vera told her they had got into conversation in the bar and both being on their own he had, in the politest and most charming way, suggested to Vera that they dine together. That was the evening preceding the day of Vera's lunch with Clara.

At the lunch next day Zoltan, at Vera's invitation, had joined their table for a pre-prandial dry martini, after which he had retired to his own.

"Such a charming man," Vera said after Zoltan had left us. "He's a Count, you know, of ancient Hungarian ancestry. The family live in a castle in the countryside south of Budapest."

As it happened, I was holding a dinner party at the villa later that week in Vera's honour and I suggested that she bring Zoltan along with her, and I asked her to provide me with his full title so that Frederick, my faithful secretary, could prepare a place setting card with his name on it. I didn't normally do named place settings for my parties, but with a distinguished Hungarian Count coming to dinner, why not? I thought.

Vera was quite right about the Count. His charm flowed as smoothly as the Danube and he was, moreover, as dashingly handsome as a matinée idol.

85

Before he and Vera left to return to La Reserve I asked him discreetly, making sure that Vera was out of earshot, whether he would like to come for a cocktail at the villa the following evening, an invitation which he accepted with both alacrity and evident pleasure.

Cocktails led on to a light supper and the light supper was followed inevitably by a trip to the bedroom.

Zoltan's sexual prowess was extraordinary. He managed to combine the energetic ardour of a young lover with the sophisticated bedroom technique of a seasoned seducer. Rarely has a man given me so much satisfaction.

Zoltan paid several more visits to the villa over the following two weeks. This all happened during a period after Clara had had a row with Louis over something quite trivial and Louis had not been down to see her for eight weeks.

However, a little while later, Louis arrived with the most beautiful Cartier bracelet for me as peace offering and all was forgiven and forgotten.

He asked me what I'd been up to in his absence and I told him all about Zoltan the Hungarian Count, carefully avoiding any mention of amorous liaisons but of course Louis saw through me.

"I suppose you slept with him?" He said, putting it as more of a statement than a question.

Well, er…

"Oh, I'm sure you did. I'm told that Zoltan is absolutely irresistible to women. Don't worry, I forgive you, though I shall have to summon the Major to come and give you another good spanking!"

Louis stayed with me at the villa, but after three weeks or so, he had to travel to London on family business, and a little while later I received a letter from him.

'My Darling Clara,

I have some amazing information about 'Zoltan', and I simply had to write you about it.

Prepare yourself for a shock!

Yesterday I met an old actor friend of mine at the Queens Elm in Chelsea.

Soon we got down to the usual banter that old friends, at least of the male species, do after a few drinks.

He asked me how many pretty girls I'd managed to seduce since we last met. He seems to believe that I'm some sort of libertine would you believe?! Naturally, I assured him that you were the only one! I told him, however, that there was presently a serial seducer at work on the French Riviera, a real Casanova, a proper Don Juan and that his name was Zoltan who claimed to be a Hungarian aristocrat.

My friend laughed out loud. It transpired that he knew 'Zoltan' very well. His real name is not Zoltan at all but Edward – 'Teddy' to his friends – and of course he's not a Count either. His father was an encyclopaedia salesman from Hatfield and his mother worked at a laundry there. Her grandparents were apparently Hungarian gypsies, which is about as close to Hungary as Teddy has ever been. My friend and Teddy worked together in the theatre for several seasons some years ago.

Ever since he was a young, Teddy had always wanted a career on the stage and he took a job as a stage hand with a touring theatre company. Soon his natural talent was recognised and he became an actor – as he'd always dreamed that he would. At first he was cast in minor parts but he quickly moved up the thespian ladder to play more important roles. Despite his humble origins, he was very good at assuming an aristocratic bearing and was often cast as a shining white knight or a roguish duke. Invariably in Christmas pantomimes he played the part of Prince Charming.

After some years of treading the boards Teddy thought that he could do better for himself if he left the theatre and played this sort of role for real, and cast himself as a Hungarian aristocrat. Nobody, he thought, would know much about the Hungarian nobility and his deception would be easier to maintain.

And very successful he's been. Deploying his good looks and 'aristocratic' charm he specialises in seducing wealthy, older women or impressionable young ones, insinuating himself into their affections and before long, he has them eating out of his hand, indulging his every wish and paying his bills. He always manages to move on before he's found out.

Clara my dear, I doubt that you will be seeing much more of Zoltan, or rather Teddy, and if you've been foolish enough to lend him money as others have done, I'm afraid you won't be seeing the return of that either.

I hope to be with you again soon.

In the meantime, just be a good girl!

With all my love, Louis'

In copying out the text of Louis's letter above I have omitted Teddy's real surname and I also have refrained from mentioning the Hungarian surname which he had assumed for the purposes of his pretence. Of course he's a rogue, but a very charming one who had given me such a good time. Just like Margot with her Hector or whoever he was, I could not contemplate betraying him.

I hoped that he'd make himself scarce before he was found out. I wished him all the best.

***

Of course one might be forgiven for thinking that most of the people Clara invited to her parties were rogues, eccentrics, serial seducers and imposters but most were in fact eminently respectable, normal folk whose identity there was no need for her to conceal but, as I read on through the book, it was the outrageous, flamboyant and often dubious characters who featured more. Evidently, she found it easier to write about them in a way which she thought would interest her readers.

It is difficult not to sound banal when writing about decent, honest respectable people – a bit like a local newspaper reporter trying to pen an article on a day when nothing much has happened…something along the following lines:

'It was reported that a record number of old ladies were helped across the road in Harrogate today, matched only by the number of umbrellas left by their owners at the public library.

Fluffy, a tortoiseshell cat reported missing last week by her owner, Mr Ernest Longbottom, was found today in the travel section of the Wise Owl Bookshop.

The rain forecast for this afternoon failed to materialise and there was only a short period of light drizzle.

All train and bus services ran on time.

There were exceptions, however.

Visits by distinguished academics, like the professor from the Sorbonne, as well as diplomats, writers, artists, and army officers, decorated for valour in the Great War, all commanded some attention.

Jean Cocteau, the French poet, artist and polymath who visited the villa on two or three occasions and whom Clara clearly admired, receives a rather longer mention. Cocteau often visited Villefranche, a place he truly loved. Indeed he lived there for a time at the Welcome Hotel on the sea front. His exquisite decoration of the interior of the Chapelle St Pierre in the town was undertaken in 1957 – long after Clara had written her book but I'm sure she would have got to see it.

***

From 1933 to late summer of 1938, Louis spent more time in the South of France, only returning to Paris for a few days each month. Furthermore, he stayed with Clara at the villa, forsaking his usual suite at the Negresco.

She had already written that he was 'The One' and it is quite clear to me that they were in love.

In 1938, however, something was to happen which changed everything. On a sultry evening at the end of August Louis returned from one of his short trips to Paris.

"I have some news, Clara," he said. "My wife is pregnant."

"Oh," I replied. "Well, congratulations, then."

This obviously came as a total surprise. I had thought that normal marital relations between Louis and Amelie, his wife, had ceased years ago and that, as Louis had always maintained, he and his wife lived separate lives. I could not help but feel a little hurt.

"Oh, I'm not the father if that's what you think. Amelie had been having an affair with another man for some considerable time."

"Well, you can hardly blame her!"

"Of course I don't blame her, though her choice of lover is a bit of a problem. But that's a complicated issue with which I shan't bore you."

"When's the baby due?"

"March next year, I believe."

"So, what happens, then?"

"I shall treat the baby as my own. Amelie and I are in complete agreement about that. It's best that I'm seen to be the father."

"I see."

"Clara, I'm afraid this means that, once this baby is born, I shan't be able to see you so much."

This was about as far as I'd got when the flight was called. I thought I'd read a bit more but fell asleep soon after take-off.

16

Home again very late, we both fell into bed without unpacking. I had a rather vivid, muddled dream in which I found myself on the terrace of the Villa Mirabeau with Gerard Belcourt and a man, who, I remembered, was called Monsieur Fifty-fifty, a well-known pimp.

'And I know what you've come for,' Monsieur Fifty-fifty said to me as we shook hands. 'A nice plump trollop to have a bit of fun with!'

'Certainly not!' I protested. 'You must be thinking of someone else.

'He says he's Clara's cousin,' Gerard said referring to me. 'But of course he could be an imposter.'

'Never mind. We're all imposters really.' Monsieur Fifty-fifty replied. 'Let's go down to the gazebo for some canoodling. I've arranged for some cheap young tarts to meet us there...'

***

On the day after our return, a Friday, there was to be a public meeting in the Church Hall about the proposals for Cloverton Hall. Donald Watson, my neighbour and chairman of the informal opposition group which I had been invited to join, suggested that we should meet up before the public meeting to discuss tactics. He suggested 4 pm at his house. As it was almost the weekend, I had decided that I would defer returning to work until Monday, so had no problem agreeing to attend.

After a fairly late breakfast Charlotte announced that she would head off to do some shopping and I decided, as it was a nice sunny day, that I would take a stroll in Cloverton Wood.

Cloverton Wood lies a little way beyond Cloverton Manor and is owned by the National Trust. It is popular with walkers and the Trust has created within it a number of marked walking trails of various lengths. There is a car park reached by a narrow lane but, as the wood is only a twenty-minute walk from our cottage there was no need for me to take the car.

I chose my favourite trail, a circular route which takes about half an hour to complete and near its end passes by a wooden hut close to the car park where tea, coffee, soft drinks and light snacks are available.

When I got to the hut I decided that I would stop for a cup of tea. One of the Trust's rangers who look after the wood happened to be there. I knew him slightly and we sat together

91

at one of the tables laid out for customers in the small clearing next to the hut, in the shade of a giant copper beech tree.

I brought up the subject of Cloverton Hall and its future.

"It's such a shame," he said. "Until a couple of months ago Lord Pendlebury had been in negotiation for the Trust to take over the Hall."

"Really?" I said, my interest immediately perking up. "I'd no idea."

"Oh, yes. I have a friend who works at the Trust's regional offices and has kept me informed. The Hall is actually in a sorry state, though you might not realize it from a distance. The roof needs completely renewing and there's a subsidence problem in the east wing. Many of the windows need replacing, the floor of the Long Gallery is sagging, the banqueting hall and much of the ground floor suffers from rising damp, the whole place needs re-wiring and there are many more problems besides."

"So I suppose the place had become too much of a burden for the family?"

"That's right. The cost of the renovations would be substantial. Lord Pendlebury approached the Trust which was prepared to acquire the property but would only pay a nominal price on the basis that we would undertake the repair and renovation works at the Trust's expense. As part of the agreement the old hunting lodge, West Lodge, near the rear entrance to the Hall, would also be refurbished at our expense for Lord and Lady Pendlebury to occupy free of rent for the rest of their lives."

"Sounds like a good deal."

"Yes. It's similar to the sort of arrangement that the Trust has come to with other former owners of heritage properties. In this case, it was good that the Trust would have two properties adjoining one another, the Hall and these woods. Visitors would be able to use the Trust's car park here, a five-minute walk from the side entrance to the Hall.

"It was all shaping up so nicely, but suddenly Lord Pendlebury broke off from the negotiations and the next we heard an application had been made to the planners to convert the Hall into a wedding venue and conference centre."

"Yes, more's the pity!"

"I understand from my friend at the office that the idea came from Sir Lawrence's brother-in-law, Lady Pendlebury's older brother who has a catering business in London."

"All this is really most interesting," I said.

We both expressed the hope that, in the light of local opposition, the planning application would be turned down.

***

I arrived slightly early for the meeting at Donald's house, the first there in fact. I have always liked Donald's house, Maple Lodge, a large Regency villa near the church and set in a big, well-kept garden with wonderful all-round views of the countryside and across the wild flower meadow towards Cloverton Hall. Somehow, for reasons I find difficult to explain, it reminded me of the Villa Mirabeau…perhaps, like Clara's villa, it was because it radiated an aura of friendliness and welcome.

There was even a gazebo, not a permanent wrought iron structure like the one at the Villa, but a temporary, stripey tented one which Donald had put up in recent days to take advantage of the spell of good weather. Still a gazebo's a gazebo.

"I thought we'd have our meeting out here in the gazebo," Donald said. "Gina's baked a nice sponge cake for us and I'm sure she'll brew up some tea. Let's go and make ourselves comfortable. I'm sure the others will be along in a moment or two."

A table and chairs had been set down in the shade of the gazebo and I chose a chair with a view looking across the meadow directly towards the eastern elevation of Cloverton Hall.

Soon we were joined by the rest of our informal committee.

"I'm pleased to tell you all," Donald began, "that there have been now thirty-five written objections lodged with Council and I expect there will be a good turn-out tonight for the meeting in the Church Hall. And a big thank you, Bob," he said, addressing a member of the committee, "for organizing the distribution of the flyers around the village. Many thanks, too, to you Geoff for helping draft the letters which we sent to the National Trust, English Heritage and the Council for the Protection of Rural England all of whom, I should add, have made very helpful written representations to the Council, copies of which they kindly sent on to me."

Before we got on to other things I thought I should report on my conversation that morning with Dan Cooper, the National Trust ranger.

"That's really most interesting," Donald said. "I don't think any of us knew about the earlier involvement of the National Trust. They don't mention it in their letter of objection. I must say I heartily agree with Dan – what a crying shame the negotiations were broken off. It would have been an ideal solution."

There was a general murmuring of agreement around the table.

"I had heard, though," Donald continued, "that the proposal for conversion to a wedding venue and conference centre came from Lord Pendlebury's brother-in-law Simon Tilson, and that he runs a company in London called Elite Catering Solutions Ltd of which he is the majority shareholder. I gather that this is the company which would manage the intended business operation.

"I have it on good authority that if planning consent is obtained Pendlebury will transfer the Hall to this company in return for an equal shareholding with Tilson and a seat on the board of directors.

"Thereafter, I gather the plan is to sell off the two farms forming part of the Cloverton Hall estate in order to raise cash towards the renovation and conversion works… hence, of course, the need to convert the meadow into a car park.

"West Lodge would be retained for occupation for Lord and Lady Pendlebury rent free, as would have been the case from what you tell us, Geoff, under the National Trust proposals."

Well at least now we knew the full picture, I thought; always good in a war to know your enemies' plans in advance.

"So far as the public meeting goes," Donald went on. "Colonel Masters as chairman of the Cloverton Residents' Association has agreed to take the chair. I believe that Lord Pendlebury himself will be there and also this chap Tilson, the brother-in -law. Mark Bridges, our local councillor, indicated that he would attend and hoped that at least one member of the planning committee would also be coming."

Tea and a home-made sponge cake duly arrived and as we refreshed ourselves we agreed between us a number of key questions to raise, allocating each one to a different member of the committee. We hoped this would stimulate a lively discussion and prompt the fullest possible public engagement in the important issues at stake.

Soon it was time for us to make our way to the church hall, only a short stroll from Donald's house.

17

On the raised stage in the Church Hall there were placed five chairs and a long table. The central chair was occupied by Colonel Masters, chosen as chairman for the evening, and he was flanked on one side by our local councillor, Mark Bridges, and a lady, Mrs. Mary Thomson, another councillor who was also member of the Planning Committee. On the other side of the chairman sat Lord Pendlebury looking, I thought, a little uneasy and, next to him, his brother-in-law Simon Tilson, all smiles.

As the large clock above the stage showed the time as 6 pm, the appointed hour for the start of the meeting, the chairman rose to his feet, welcomed members of the public and made the necessary introductions of those with him on the stage.

"I'm glad to see so many residents of our village here this evening," he said in a rich, booming voice. "The purpose of this meeting is to give you all the opportunity to express your views on the proposals for Cloverton Hall referred to in the recent planning application submitted by Lord Pendlebury. However, I would first call upon Mr. Simon Tilson, whose company Elite Catering Solutions Ltd. will, I understand, be managing the enterprise if permission is granted and who would like to say a few words about the proposals."

Springing to his feet and moving a little closer to the edge of the stage, Tilson thanked the chairman and began with a short account of his company's history and the nature of its business activities, including his own background in catering and events management. Next, in some detail he explained the proposals for the conversion of Cloverton Hall and certain outbuildings for the purpose of a wedding venue and conference centre and the various works that would be required, laying particular emphasis on the repairs and renovations to the Hall. Repairs that would be necessary whatever happened.

"So, ladies and gentlemen, assuming we are successful in obtaining planning approval, the works we shall be undertaking will be as much about the much-needed restoration of the Hall as a Grade-I listed building of great historical importance as about the conversion and other works required to prepare for our exciting new enterprise. Works, I should add, which will not in any way alter or intrude upon any of the main areas of architectural interest in the Hall. For example, the grand staircase, banqueting hall, and minstrels' gallery. I'm pleased to say that the Hall will be open to members of the public to visit free every Sunday afternoon except when there is a function.

"I would also like to add that Lord and Lady Pendlebury will continue to reside at West Lodge thereby preserving the historic connection of the Pendlebury family with Cloverton Hall, the village and local area."

Mr. Tilson was well-spoken and articulate. He came across as a posh, self-assured, suave sort of character, perhaps a little too suave. One certainly couldn't fairly describe him as a 'West-end wide-boy'. Perhaps 'West-end smooth boy' would be a more fitting description.

Looked at objectively from a PR perspective, I would have to admit that so far, he was doing a good job. Then everything began to unravel. He committed the cardinal error of misjudging his audience. He had not done his research and plainly thought he was addressing an audience of country bumkins and old fogeys whom he could take for a proverbial ride. Well, he was in for a rude awakening.

"I don't think you realise, ladies and gentlemen, quite how lucky you are," he intoned, condescendingly. "Once we commence trading, your village will benefit from an enormous boost to trade and many new employment opportunities. A new buzz, a new vitality, a fresh vibrancy will rejuvenate the village high street!"

Oh, I thought to myself, how people of this sort love the words 'buzz' 'vital' and 'vibrant. As a PR man I've been just as guilty. But the village high street surely didn't need any rejuvenation. Cloverton was neither a dead commuter village nor a trendy destination for young hipsters, it was properly functioning village with a natural charm and a life of its own, and that's the way I'm sure most of us wanted to keep it.

There were a few polite claps but otherwise the audience remained largely silent. Not many showed any sign of being much impressed. Donald, who was sitting next to me, gave me a meaningful sideways glance and a little smile.

Tilson thanked the chairman and with a look of smug satisfaction resumed his seat.

The chairman then invited questions and comments from the floor.

I was the first on my feet to question the promised boost in trade.

"We don't do so badly here in Cloverton as things stand," I said. "I wonder what sectors of the local economy Mr. Tilson thinks would benefit so much more from what he calls 'his exciting new enterprise' at the Hall?"

"We anticipate that there could be upwards of 200 guests at many of our weddings," Tilson replied, without bothering to rise from his seat. "Dwarfing your existing tourist trade."

"But they'll surely spend their time mainly at the Hall, won't they? Of course, a few might drop into the pub for a quick pint before the marriage service. That may be a welcome addition to the pub's takings but hardly a fantastic boost to village trade and probably a source of irritation to the regulars who might find it more difficult to get to the bar!"

This raised a few modest titters around the room.

"I was hoping for your assurance," I continued, addressing Tilson directly, "that your company would be sourcing all of its supplies from local shops and farms but, as you haven't given any such assurance, I assume that you intend to source from your regular suppliers, probably able to offer you cheaper deals."

"Well, it's er, early days," Tilson replied a little defensively. "We have yet to decide our policy on such matters."

"So, no assurance then?"

"The hospitality businesses in Cloverton will certainly benefit," Tilson went on – hastily passing on from the question of sourcing supplies. "When all the works are completed Cloverton Hall will be able to offer twenty bedrooms overall, some in the Hall itself and some in the converted stable block. The concept is that, for weddings, we would aim to accommodate the bride and groom and close friends and family members, but other guests wanting to stay locally would need to make their own arrangements. There would accordingly be an overflow of people seeking accommodation. The same goes for business conferences."

I was ready for this one.

"The pub has ten bedrooms and there are five traditional B&Bs which have between three and five bedrooms each. I gather that their occupancy rates are pretty good except in the depths of winter, though I'm sure that they'd be pleased to fill the odd vacancy. But this would hardly likely add up to the 'enormous boost to trade' you refer to. If there are a substantial number of overflow guests they're all likely to use the larger town or country house hotels in the wider area, of which there are many."

"But you're forgetting Airbnbs," Tilson cut in.

"Yes, I concede. A few residents do indeed let rooms in their houses on the Airbnb platform and wedding guests staying overnight might find this useful if there are vacancies. Lettings no doubt greatly help householders with the payment of their mortgages and household expenses. However, it's difficult to see how any of this would have a really dramatic impact on the local economy and, frankly, I doubt many other residents would want to start new hospitality businesses in the village".

Time for me to finish, I thought.

"Let's face it." I concluded, with a final rhetorical flourish. "Whatever you get up to at the Hall is unlikely to pave the streets of Cloverton with gold!"

I sat down to not quite tumultuous applause but to much longer and louder clapping than for Mr. Tilson who, for the first time, I was pleased to note appeared a little flustered.

Next up, Donald tested the claim that there would be an increase in local employment.

Tilson did his best to prevaricate but, after Donald had persisted in pressing him, this boiled down to a few jobs for waiters, junior kitchen staff and a couple of receptionists. Apart from the receptionists the jobs were part-time only, though Tilson made a vague suggestion that there could be more senior full-time positions in the course of time.

"Nothing would appear to justify Mr. Tilson's claims with regard to employment." Donald correctly concluded, adding the killer fact that "Cloverton doesn't actually have a current problem with unemployment in any case."

Another member of our committee raised the issue of the wild flower meadow:

"The loss of the meadow would be an absolute tragedy. Owing to modern farming methods, traditional meadows are rare today and of great ecological value. It is one of the local landscape features which make our village such a special place."

This was met with a gale of applause and cries of 'hear, hear!' from all round the audience.

Someone whom I recognised as a surveyor with the local estate agency in the High Street, spoke next.

"Even if, and I agree with the last speaker that this would be a tragedy, most of the meadow becomes a car park there might still not be enough parking on site for a big wedding or conference. This could lead to the surrounding roads, which are all very narrow, becoming clogged with parked cars, in particular Church Lane and the lane leading to the National Trust car park at Cloverton Wood."

A stout, middle-aged woman at the back of the hall who caught the Chairman's eye expressed concern that our local church, St Barnabas, might be monopolised by clients of the new business wanting a traditional church wedding, at the expense of couples from Cloverton and the wider local area.

The issue of noise from wedding receptions was a concern for several speakers especially if it were to continue late into the evening and involved loud music, a fear which, from the volume of 'hear, hears!', was generally shared.

Many others in the hall that evening clamoured to raise their own concerns or to express their agreement with other speakers. Of all the issues the ones which seemed to concern people most were noise, traffic congestion, overflow parking and, above all, the loss of the wild flower meadow. The token area of meadow that would be left near the church was not regarded as much of a consolation.

The meeting went on for much longer than I had anticipated. Eventually the chairman was able to bring matters to a close, after allowing Donald to have the final say.

Deftly, like the good lawyer he was, Donald briefly summarised all the issues which had been raised, and concluded that:

"The benefits, if any, which might accrue to the village from the use of Cloverton Hall as a wedding venue and conference centre would clearly be more than out-weighed by the problems, disadvantages and loss of amenity resulting from it."

After the meeting a few of us gathered in the forecourt outside the church hall for a post mortem and were joined by Colonel Masters. There was no sign of Lord Pendlebury or his brother-in-law Simon Tilson.

"Obviously sneaked off with their tails between their legs," Colonel Masters sneered disdainfully.

We all, even cautious old Donald, felt pretty pleased about the way the meeting had gone and trusted that the councillors who had been present would report back accurately to the planning committee the strength of feeling in the village and our justified concerns.

We were just about to disperse when our local councillor, Mark Bridges, came over to speak to us.

"Well, that should surely have put paid to this planning application once and for all," I said, addressing Mr Bridges.

"I shouldn't count on it if I were you," he replied.

"Well, what was the view of your colleague who, I gather, sits on the planning committee?" Donald asked.

"Non-committal, though I'm sure she'll report the concerns expressed. Look, don't get me wrong, I'm entirely on your side and will do what I can but many of the councillors on the planning committee have expressed support for the application."

"But why on earth?" I asked.

"Because it's a policy of the Council to encourage new business in rural areas, to create employment and save villages from becoming dormitories for nearby cities and bigger towns."

"A good policy," Donald agreed. "But it shouldn't be a blanket one. Cloverton is not just a dormitory, it's a thriving village in its own right. Nor is there any significant unemployment here, nor lack of jobs for young people. We've a busy high street with a mix of retail, hospitality and other uses, a popular pub and, close by, a farm shop, a renowned riding school and not to forget the craft workshops recently set up in our famous tithe barn."

"Yes, I know. I'm with you entirely but the thing is that in terms of 'the Rural Business Initiative', as the policy's called, it's not been a good year. There were some quite promising opportunities but in the end except for a few small start-ups they all came to nothing. Then along came Lord Pendlebury with his wedding venue and conference centre proposal and many councillors think it would look bad if it was turned down. It might appear that the Council was not taking the policy seriously.

"Also the company, Elite Catering Solutions, indicated that if all goes well they plan to relocate their head office to a new building to be constructed in the yard area behind the stable block. It would be a great coup for the Council for a London business to relocate their head office to our area."

"So, what you're saying then, is that local opinion may not count for much. It may all boil down to politics."

"Doesn't it always?"

***

It didn't look good and though Charlotte tried hard to cheer me up, I was in a depressed sort of mood as I went to bed that evening.

To take my mind off things I read some more of Clara's book.

Louis was now a much less frequent visitor and Clara plainly was missing him. The parties went on as usual.

The news from Germany continued to look ominous and there were stories of dreadful things happening to minority groups: gypsies, the mentally retarded and, above all, Jews.

Just after the signing of the Munich Agreement in September 1938 between Britain, France, Italy and Nazi Germany, Clara had attended a dinner party at the Bentham villa in Menton. Sir Henry had plainly not thought much of it.

"Shameful Agreement," he said. "Anyone who seriously thinks that that Hitler will be satisfied with the take-over of the Sudetenland and

104

that will be an end to his territorial ambitions is sadly deluding himself.
It will not mean 'peace in our time' as Chamberlain seems to believe.
Sooner or later, there'll be a war."

There were those at the party who disagreed but Clara was more than half convinced that Sir Henry was right, and in March 1939 when German troops marched into Prague she decided that the time had come to return to England and began to make preparations to leave.

I'd now reached the final chapter but since my sleeping pill began to take effect, that would have to wait.

18

Saturday again. I reflected that the last Saturday that I'd spent at home was the one before our holiday in France, the day I'd bought Clara's book. So much had happened in those few weeks. It seemed to me that I'd not just returned from a different country but, reading the book, a different world: Clara's world, and I still had a little way to go with it.

As usual I awoke early, Charlotte still asleep beside me. I stealthily crept out of bed to draw the curtains a little to see what sort of day it was.

Whilst a pale sky with a hint of blue in it promised sunshine later, a low-lying mist spread over the landscape. The view of distant hills was obscured and only a little of the near foreground was visible – although I could just detect the ghostly outline of the spire of St. Barnabas church rising through the mist.

A horrible vision floated unbidden into my mind, a vision of the mist suddenly lifting off to reveal not a glorious wild flower meadow but serried ranks of Range Rovers and BMWs.

"But, darling, we've just got a new BMW ourselves," Charlotte said later over breakfastt after I'd told her of my ghastly day dream. "And you seem so pleased with it."

"Don't tease me, Charlotte. I've nothing against BMWs or Land Rovers for that matter but they don't belong in that meadow!"

"I know, dear. I was only trying to cheer you up!"

***

Not in the least cheered up and without any of my usual enthusiasm for it I set out after breakfast, creature of habit that I am, to take my customary walk to buy the newspaper at the village shop.

The morning mist had by then cleared and it had become warm and sunny. I couldn't bear to look at the meadow as I passed by, fearing that it might soon be lost. I couldn't bear not to look either.

And of course it looked more beautiful than ever: a riot of colour with oxeye daisies, red clover, buttercups and cowslips along with many other species of meadow flowers and grasses. Chaffinches, blue tits and yellow wagtails flew just above the grass, dipping and diving in search of insects and I spotted at least four species of butterfly: cabbage whites, common blues, peacocks and red admirals.

I didn't linger but returned home with the paper.

Charlotte was waiting for me in the hallway.

"Oh God, did I forget to buy the lamb chops or something?" I asked nervously.

"No, no, nothing like that," she replied to my relief. "It's just something I forgot to tell you."

"Oh, yes?"

"Well, when I was packing my case just before we left France, I looked under the bed to check that nothing had got pushed under it. I always do that ever since that time I left a pair of my shoes there."

"And you found something?"

"Yes I did. It was a page from Clara's book."

"How do you know it was Clara's book?"

"Because while you were out getting the paper just now, I checked the copy you're reading and there's an identical page there, page 283"

"I see. So that proves beyond doubt that I was right. Copies of the book were indeed switched. This page must have become detached when my original copy of the book fell on the floor during the night. Separated from the book it must have wafted under the bed."

"Yes, that's the only explanation. I'm sorry Geoff, I meant to tell you about this before but I was in such a hurry at the time. I just stuffed the page into my suitcase and forgot all about it until now."

"Never mind, you're forgiven. Can I see it?"

"Of course. Here it is."

The page, page 283/4, came right from the end of the book. Page 283 was a page of acknowledgements, thanking those who'd helped in some way: editors and proof-readers (including her secretary Frederick Latham), her literary agent, publishers and a few others including Margot Bentham and Louis (again without surname).

"Oh, one other thing," Charlotte continued. "You will see that there's some scribble on the reverse of the page, that's to say page 284."

Page 284 was blank of print but someone had written all over it. This 'scribble' as Charlotte dismissively referred to it consisted of a list of names written in very small neat handwriting. There were the names or pseudonyms of all the people in Clara's book whose identity for one reason or another she had wanted to conceal to 'spare their blushes' – as Margot Bentham had put it in her preface – and no doubt to appease her publisher who might otherwise have been concerned with claims for libel. Opposite each name was written the full name of the person concerned, sometimes with further details.

I sat down on the seat in the hallway and read the first name on the list and the full name given.

Louis. Louis Belcourt

So Gerard was a relation. Indeed more than likely, Louis's grandson. I might have guessed as much.

There were about fifteen people in all; a few women, mostly men. I recognised most of them from the book but it was an entry towards the end of the list that caused me to jump to my feet in complete astonishment. It read:

Hector – John Forbes impersonating Lord Hector Pendlebury of Cloverton Hall.

"Good God!" I said to Charlotte's evident bemusement, as the implications exploded in my mind like a dozen champagne corks popping in rapid succession. This was dynamite.

The man introduced by Margot was indeed an imposter whose real name was John Forbes masquerading as Lord Hector Pendlebury.

So if George, Lawrence's father, was the son of this imposter, John Forbes, then George was not a Pendlebury at all. His real name was Forbes. By the same token, Lawrence would not be the current Lord Pendlebury but Lawrence Forbes. Therefore, he would have no legal title to Cloverton Hall, no right even to live there let alone any right to convert it into a wedding venue and desecrate the wild flower meadow.

Of course the assumption might be wrong. George *could* have been the son of the real Lord Pendlebury if he'd still been about, and Lawrence *could* still be the legitimate heir to the barony. But if Lawrence was the grandson of an imposter this would be the end of all our problems. It clearly merited serious enquiry and the man to deal with it was my wily old lawyer friend Donald.

"What is it, Geoff? Tell me," Charlotte asked, exasperated.

"I'll explain it all in just a moment, but first I must call Donald."

I was just about to make my way to the telephone in my study when it rang.

Charlotte got there first and picked up.

"It's Gerard for you."

"Gerard?"

"Gerard Belcourt…you remember?" She said, passing me the handset.

"Hello," I said, surprised. What did he want?

"Is that Mr. Momford?"

"Speaking."

"I wonder if I could come and see you. There's something I'd like to talk to you about and frankly I think I owe you an apology and an explanation."

"I'm not sure that I understand but I should be very pleased to see you. I shall be in my office in Birmingham all next week. If you'd like to phone my secretary, I'm sure something can be arranged. Perhaps we could have lunch together, I'll give you the number…"

"Actually, I was hoping we could meet this morning."

"This morning?!"

"Yes, you see I'm staying at the Hall with the Pendleburys."

"I think you mean the Forbes," I said, speaking slowly and deliberately, laying emphasis on the name 'Forbes'.

"Ah…so you know, then… You *do* have the list."

Well, well. That was significant. Belcourt had not sought to deny the Forbes' connection. In fact, the way he put it was tantamount to an admission.

"Yes, I have the list."

"I can be with you in twenty minutes. Would that be all right?"

"Fine. Look forward to seeing you."

As it was still warm and sunny we decided to have our meeting in the garden. Charlotte brought us out some coffee.

"So you must be Louis's grandson?" I asked.

"Yes, indeed I am. Louis bought Villa Mirabeau from Clara in 1958. My father inherited on Louis's death and my father transferred it into my name ten years ago."

"Thank you. That's interesting to know. By the way, would you mind if Charlotte stayed with us? I know she'd like to hear what you have to say."

"No problem, Geoff. You don't mind if I call you that?"

"Not at all, Gerard. And here, by the way, is the page with the list."

Gerard took his time to go through it as we sipped our coffee, before passing it back to me. I explained how the page had come adrift and how and when it was found.

"Incidentally, was it you," I asked, "who got someone to switch the books?"

"Yes, I'm afraid it was and I most sincerely apologise."

"And it was the same someone, pretending again to be a plumber, who made a subsequent intrusion?"

"Yes, it was. Actually, Pierre *is* in fact a plumber but I have to admit that that plumbing was not the purpose of his visit any more than it was the first time. But before you say anything, please allow me to explain the background to all this."

"Please do."

"Well to begin at the beginning as they say, Clara's book was published in 1947 and sold well, being especially popular of course with the many people who were friends or had been guests at her parties over the years before the war. It became popular with many others too, as her reputation as a leading socialite had spread far and wide not only in France but England too.

"However, later that year individuals mentioned in the book, who are referred to by their first names only or pseudonyms to protect their identity, started to receive letters from a free-lance journalist called David Merrick, threatening to publish their full names in a review of that he was proposing to submit to the press. Unless, that is, they each coughed up a substantial sum of money. It was naked blackmail.

"Merrick was married to a French woman and resided partly in London and partly in Nice. He wrote articles and reviews for both the English and French press as well as being a regular contributor to an English language weekly on the French Riviera. He was a well-known figure among the English ex-pat community, though not well-liked. In fact he was widely regarded, quite rightly, as a slippery and unscrupulous character – a thoroughly nasty piece of work.

"It was soon discovered that it was Frederick Latham, Clara's secretary, who had written out the list of the names in a copy of the book and sold it to Merrick for cash.

"Frederick was of course in a unique position as her secretary and one who had also been helping to edit her book, to know the names of all those whose identity, for one reason or another, Clara had sought to protect. Indeed, even if peoples' names were not on the guest list for a party or mentioned in Clara's correspondence, he would make it his business to find out who they were.

"It was Louis, my grandfather, who suspected Frederick and tracked him down to a bar in Nice where he was working part-time; there he forced him to admit his treachery.

"Frederick had spent the war in Leeds with his widowed mother but returned to France in 1947, just about the time of publication of the book. He had got another job as tutor to children of a wealthy ex-pat English family at Cap d'Antibes but it didn't last and, being short of money, he did the deal with Merrick.

"He insisted that he knew nothing of Merrick's intention to use the list for blackmail but only as information for a newspaper article or book review. In a brazen outburst he said that he felt no guilt at all for what he'd done. So far as he was concerned, all the people on the list were immoral or corrupt and deserved to be exposed. This was utterly hypocritical. My grandfather discovered that Frederick was not as unlucky or hard done by as he pretended but was himself both a liar and seducer.

"The stories he told were all untrue. He had never had a young wife who died of Spanish Flu. Indeed, he was never married. He didn't lose his job at the school in Leicestershire because it closed as he had asserted, but because he had been found in bed with the headmaster's wife. He didn't lose his position as private tutor to the daughter of wealthy Italian parents in Turin because the girl was sent to a Swiss finishing school, but because, taking advantage of her youth and innocence, he had wickedly seduced her.

"Finally, he had lost his most recent tutoring job at Cap d'Antibes when he had been found hopelessly drunk in the wine cellar of his employer's house, having consumed two bottles of the latter's finest red burgundy.

"If Merrick was a thoroughly bad lot, Frederick Latham was a snake in the grass of the most slithery variety!"

"Good God," I said. "What a story! So the book I bought in the charity shop here in Cloverton was the very book, containing the list of names, that Frederick sold to this man Merrick and you wanted to get hold of."

"Yes."

"But what made you think that it was that same book?"

"I was just coming to that."

"Sorry, please do continue."

"Well, when Clara heard about the blackmail she was obviously most upset and at my grandfather Louis's suggestion, she contacted Frank Duncan. He was the one, you will recall from the book, who negotiated the purchase of Villa Mirabeau on Clara's behalf, the one who Louis described as 'very good at fixing things'. She asked him to negotiate a deal with Merrick to stop any publication of the list.

"Frank and his wife had spent the war in South Africa but by the time Clara contacted him he had returned to his home in Monte Carlo and was happy to accept the assignment. Always exceptionally well-informed about local affairs, Frank knew of Merrick and the sort of man he was, and happily he had discovered through his network of local contacts one or two dubious dealings in which Merrick was implicated and which he would certainly not wish the world to know about. Quite soon a deal was done on, let us say, reasonable terms, if any deal with a blackmailer can be described as reasonable.

"Merrick was paid a modest sum of money for the book and it was understood that if he was ever to reveal the identity of anyone on the list or attempted to extract more money by threatening to do so, then the world would know all about his involvement in the dubious dealings which Frank had uncovered. I might add that Clara characteristically paid the money out of her own pocket, including Frank's fee and expenses, without seeking any contribution from anyone else. Frederick had been her secretary and she felt responsible.

"Frank was supposed to have destroyed the book or at least the offending page but, according to Louis, he was a man who liked to store up information about people and their affairs,in case it might one day be useful to him. Gathering information to him was as collecting stamps to a stamp collector. You may recall from the book that he regarded 'information as power'?

In Louis's view, to expect Frank to dispose of information would be like asking a philatelist to burn a stamp album.

"Then, suddenly, you turn up at the villa revealing that you had acquired a copy of Clara's book and that the previous owner was Matthew Duncan, Frank's grandson. Of course it might not have been the same copy as the one with the list in it but it seemed a distinct possibility. I felt that I had to prevent any chance that the list might find its way into the public domain.

"Not without some reluctance, I decided action had to be taken so I came to an arrangement with Pierre – a friend of Marie our housekeeper – to take your book and substitute for it another copy. Pierre had no difficulty in finding out where you were staying. We had a rough idea anyway. The hope was that you wouldn't be aware of the change if you hadn't yet noticed the list."

"Indeed I hadn't." I said. "It's right at the end of the book."

"If we'd stolen the book I thought you might realise that it was my doing and start asking awkward questions. In any case, I'm not a thief and stealing went against the grain. I would feel better about it, I thought, if you were provided with a substitute copy. Fortunately, I have several copies at the villa."

"But of course, you still didn't get quite what you wanted. The page with the list wasn't there."

"Quite so. I remember you saying that the book was in perfect condition but when Pierre delivered it to me after the switching, I noticed that it was damaged. Pierre swore that that it was not he who had caused it."

"And indeed," I said, "it was because the book switched for my copy *was* in perfect condition that I thought something odd had happened."

"Well in view of what you had told me about the condition of your copy of the book, I assumed correctly that it must have been damaged *after* you first came to the villa and that there was a good chance that the missing page might be somewhere in the apartment. So I persuaded Pierre – for an extra reward – to go back and see if he could find it. And indeed he might well have done so but you came home too soon.

"When he heard you coming up the stairs, he knew you were hardly likely to believe a repeat of the story that he'd come to mend a leaking pipe. He panicked and made a run for it, bumping into you in the process and causing you to fall. Poor Pierre meant you no harm and is deeply apologetic…as indeed am I."

"Oh, as you've been so honest with us and apologised we forgive you, don't we dear?" Charlotte said.

Both she and Gerard looked in my direction and I nodded in agreement. What else could I do?

"That's very kind of you. Now, you might ask what was the point? Who would really be concerned today if it was revealed that their father or grandfather had got up to something a bit naughty in the 1930s? And of course in most cases you'd be right. No-one would. Sometimes, however, the past casts a long shadow and what people did many years ago can have repercussions even in the present day."

"True enough," I said.

"Let me give you some examples of people on the list," Gerard continued, "whose descendants might be prejudiced in some way by the disclosure of their ancestors' identity."

"Do go ahead, please"

"Take Gino and Julie whose real names as the list reveals, were Gianpiero Lucarelli and Jacqueline Pennard. Both married in the 1950s into most respectable families. Gianpiero's only son is a bishop in the Roman Catholic church while Jacqueline's eldest daughter is a professor of moral philosophy and the chair of governors at a leading private girls' school.

"I happen to know Bishop Paolo Lucarelli quite well, a good man and a staunch upholder of traditional Christian values. He is well aware of the sort of life his father led and would be severely embarrassed if the truth about him ever became public knowledge. And I dare say Jacqueline's daughter would suffer a similar embarrassment if her mother's racy behaviour was to become widely known."

"I can understand that."

"Then there's Zoltan or rather Teddy. You will have seen that his real name was Edward Prosser and that he styled himself as Count Zoltan Varady. And I'm sure you recall Louis's letter to Clara from London with the full facts – a letter which I have no doubt Frederick would have seen.

'Teddy duly made himself scarce before he was found out, disappearing from the Riviera eventually to re-surface in New York after the war where he married an American heiress. His eldest son, now in his mid-seventies, continues in his father's footsteps and also calls himself Count Varady. Whether he really believes it or not I simply don't know.

"In any event, he is apparently very popular with the Hungarian ex-pat community in the Brooklyn area and is the founder and patron of a charity providing support for orphaned children of Hungarian and East European descent. I can't believe that any real good would come of exposing him as a fake."

"No, I suppose not," I agreed.

"And of course," Gerard went on, "there's the case of 'the Spanking Major' whose full name as disclosed was Major Roger Waverley. His grandson is enjoying a very promising military career with high expectations of future promotion. He also happens to be my son-in-law.

"Even if his career prospects were unaffected, you can but imagine the consequences if his grandfather's fondness for spanking ladies' bottoms was to become generally known. What would life be like in the officers' mess – the smirks, the jokes, the innuendos without end?

"I should add, too, that Major Waverley's grand-daughter is a member of parliament. Again, can you not envisage the sniggering and tittering that would inevitably break out every time she visited the Commons tea room?

"Would you really want to subject these good people to such indignities?"

"Certainly not!"

"And on a more serious level," Gerard continued, "take Tobias, as Clara called him, whose real name you may have noted from the list was Piers Parminter. Frederick, I see, not only provided his full name but even refers to his business of 'Parminter Fine Art Gallery' of Bond St, London.

"Clara, you will remember, refers to the rumour that Piers sometimes sold copies of works of art as if they were originals. If this was ever to come out you may picture, if you'll forgive the pun, the reaction of the many descendants of people who bought paintings from Piers in the twenties and thirties – and subsequent buyers. Is the Corot or the Munnings or the Matisse adorning the walls of dining rooms, grand staircases or drawing rooms in town mansions or country houses really an original or is it a fake?

"Piers of course is no longer alive but the business 'Parminter Fine Art Gallery', a highly respected firm, still exists and remains to this day in the ownership of members of the Parminter family, one of whom happens to be an old friend of mine. Even though these things may have happened many years ago what effect, do you imagine, might it have on the firm's reputation if the founder himself, after whom the firm is named, was suspected of selling forged art? At worst there might even be legal liabilities."

"Not a good situation, I suppose."

"But this was only a rumour, remember. The art world has always been full of gossip, some of it no doubt malicious, put about by business rivals. Would you want to ruin the reputation of a good business, not to mention the current blameless members of the Parminter family and set hares running all for the sake of a very old rumour?"

"I suppose not."

"On an even more serious level, at least so far as I'm concerned, there's the case of Louis, whom I call my grandfather, though he was not my real grandfather.

"Nobody knew the state of Louis's marriage, namely that he and Amelie my grandmother, though fond of one another, lived essentially separate lives. To avoid a scandal Louis and Amelie always behaved very discreetly and on the surface their marriage appeared a normal and happy one.

"Nor does anyone in the family now know, except for my wife, that Louis was not the father of Amelie's child, her only child, as she had no other children. That child was of course my father. To make matters worse his true father, my grandmother's lover, was her second cousin – the black sheep of the family, a crooked banker sent to prison for embezzlement.

"It's true that Louis was known to travel frequently to Nice where he had business interests in property and shipping but no-one in the family knew about his relationship with Clara. That, indeed, remains the case today.

"If the truth came out there would be the most terrible family furore.

"Worse still, it might even affect my entitlement to certain legacies and inheritances. There'd be bad blood and years of legal wrangling. Would you really want to precipitate such an outcome?"

"Not really, no."

"Very good. I thank you for that. Perhaps you can now understand why it would be the best for all concerned if this list was destroyed in case it should ever get into the wrong hands – the tabloid press or someone who might possibly see an opportunity for blackmail."

"Yes, but let us not forget," I said, in case Gerard had in mind to gloss over it, "one further case – that of John Forbes and his impersonation of Lord Hector Pendlebury and, more to the point, the implications so far as Lawrence is concerned. If his father George was not a Pendlebury then neither is Lawrence and he'd have had no right to inherit Cloverton Hall, because neither his grandfather or father had any legal title to it."

"Of course that's quite true. The wretched Frederick would have known about John Forbes' impersonation of Lord Hector Pendlebury from the letter which, if you recall, he was asked to draft to the British Consul, though it was never actually sent. However, I'm sure he never knew the full story. Perhaps, you will allow me to tell you?"

"Please do."

"Hector Pendlebury was in the Colonial Service in Kenya but resigned in 1923 when he acquired a tea plantation in the Kenyan uplands. The timing could not have been better as commercialization of tea production in Kenya was about to take off and tea planting become extremely profitable. Hector decided that he would stay in Kenya to manage the business.

"In December 1934, Hector's father died of tuberculosis and Hector succeeded to the title and to the ownership of Cloverton Hall. He decided that he must return to England. The plantation was sold and in the spring of 1935 he began the long journey home in the company of John Forbes, whom he had appointed as his chief steward to assist with the management of the plantation as the business grew. They had become very close friends and Hector had promised to grant him a tenancy of one of the farms forming part of the Cloverton Hall estate.

"The journey would take them from the port of Mombasa in Kenya through the Suez Canal to Port Said, from there to Genoa and thence overland and across the channel to England.

"Sadly, Hector, now Lord Pendlebury, having inherited the title on the demise of his father, became ill with malaria on the first leg of the journey and by the time the ship docked at Port Said he was dead. As he lay dying in his cabin he begged John, upon whom he looked as a brother, to take his name and assume his identity. Hector was his father's only child and there were no other living relatives capable of succeeding to the Pendlebury title which would accordingly die out on his death.

"Hector had been away from England for many years. Nobody there would remember him well and John was about the same age and remarkably similar in facial and overall appearance. It was very unlikely that anyone would see through the deception.

"John was reluctant at first but in the end out of loyalty to the man who had become his closest friend, he agreed to the plan. A swift exchange of passports – job done!

"This was the story, at least, that John told George his son, Lawrence's father and neither I – nor Lawrence for that matter – can see reason to doubt it. Would it not be best to let sleeping dogs lie?"

"Lie, perhaps, being the operative word!"

"Well, I grant you the situation is somewhat irregular but what good would really become of revealing the truth?"

"Maybe so, but there is the matter of Lawrence's proposal to convert the Hall into a wedding venue and conference centre which almost everyone in the village opposes for very good reasons. If the truth becomes known, that Lawrence has no legitimate claim to the Hall or right to do anything with it… that would be an end to the matter much to my and everyone else's relief."

"I understand entirely and, frankly, I believe Lawrence was put up to this idea by his wife and brother-in-law."

"I see. Not that it makes any difference."

"Look, Geoff," Gerard said after pausing for a few moments "Would you stay your hand, do nothing for a day or so? Let me speak to Lawrence about this. It would be better coming from me."

"Well all right, but if Lawrence doesn't ditch this proposal and withdraw the planning application, I shall have to take the necessary action."

"Understood. But if Lawrence plays ball, will you promise me to destroy the list?"

"I promise."

After thanking Charlotte for the coffee, Gerard stood up to leave. As he walked down the short path to the garden gate, he stopped for a moment and turned.

"Next time you come to France," he said, "you must both come for dinner at Villa Mirabeau.v 20

I think it's what your Cousin Clara would have expected."

19

Monday morning and back to work.

My secretary had only just finished bringing me up to date with all the routine stuff that had happened during my absence in France, when I received a call from Donald Watson. He seemed unusually excited for a lawyer and a man of placid temperament.

I've just heard from Colonel Masters who received a hand-delivered letter from Lord Pendlebury this morning, addressed to him as Chairman of the Cloverton Residents' Association. Guess what it says."

"I've really no idea."

"It says that he has decided to withdraw his planning application. The proposed conversion of Cloverton Hall for use as a wedding venue and conference centre will not now proceed. His decision, he says in the letter, was motivated by the clear strength of feeling of local residents expressed at Friday's meeting in the church hall. He goes on to say that he intends now to resume previous discussions with the National Trust in relation to the Hall's future."

"Good God," I said trying to sound surprised. "That's absolutely wonderful news!"

"Yes, and I think it's time for a party, a victory celebration! I suggest we meet up this evening, say 6.30 at the pub with the other members of our little committee for a few drinks. I'll ask the pub to lay on a simple buffet."

"Good idea, Donald. I'll look forward to it. See you there."

***

My first action on returning home that evening, before setting forth to the pub for 'the victory celebration', was to visit my study to pick up the loose page with the list. I took one last look at it before tearing it into shreds and depositing it in the waste paper basket. I had not only fulfilled my promise to Gerard but I firmly believed that this too would have been Clara's wish.

Over the weekend I had reached the final chapter of the book, in which Clara amidst all her preparations to leave, decided to hold one last party. It was held on a lovely mild April evening and was a grand, no-expense-spared occasion: full evening dress, jazz band and dancing into the small hours. Everyone must have known that this would be Clara's last party but no one wanted to believe it. There was a resolute jollity about it, a compelling desire to keep the fun going, to keep the tears at bay.

I had only a little left to read. In a way I was reluctant to finish it. Finishing a book that you've enjoyed, as many who like reading would attest, is like waving good-bye to an old friend or in my case a relative, to whom I felt close though I had never met her.

Climbing into bed that evening in a fairly happy state after 'the victory celebration' at the pub, I began to read the last couple of pages.

A week after her final party, Clara closed up the Villa Mirabeau and set off for England on the Train Bleu determined, as always, to do things in style.

At last, I came to the end, the final paragraph:

> The period during which I lived at the Villa Mirabeau was a lull between two terrible storms, a period which was neither an epilogue to the world which ended with the start of the Great War in 1914, nor a prologue to the world yet to come but an era of desperate gaiety, time for a party, a long, long party when the champagne continued to flow and the band to play despite the woes of the great depression and the sinister clouds of a new war looming on the horizon. But I would not have missed it, not for anything.

✳

Also by Tim Davidson

(Formerly *The Bloomsbury Manuscript*)

Servants, Masters and Rogues Music critic Hugo Belcher, in twenty-first century London, is a charming rogue who, forever short of money, plans to marry a wealthy young heiress. Meanwhile, Sandra Grisewood, a bright working-class girl, moves to London where she hopes one day to realise her dream of becoming an opera singer. Born in eighteenth-century Prague, music teacher Antonin Vasylicek, another rogue and charmer, flees to England to evade his creditors and escape a scandal. Their separate lives are, however, related in various ways, not least the discovery of the score of an opera, based on Carlo Goldoni's comic play 'The Servant of Two Masters', which a renowned musicologist believes could be a lost Mozart opera. *There is an element of truth which provided the inspiration for this book, namely that Mozart was indeed writing or intending to write a German opera based on Goldoni's play, for which a letter to his father dated 5 February 1783 provides evidence, but no score has ever come to light.*

Time for Another? A fusion of novel and short stories. George, Tom, Desmond and the Colonel are regulars at the back bar of the Sloop Inn. They delight in hearing stories related by visitors to the bar whom they have managed to engage in conversation: stories of love, infatuation, surprise and deception, tales with happy endings and tales ending in catastrophe. The regulars, too, themselves become involved in a disturbing story of their own.

Out of a Pale Blue Sky William Wilkins is a history teacher at a minor public school in Gloucestershire and only son of a successful art dealer. Life in this quiet educational backwater is pleasant and easy-going, ideally suited to William's unadventurous nature. His agreeable life and future prospects, however, are suddenly overturned by a series of events coming without warning out of a pale blue sky.

The Girl from Milan The lives of a Bristol antique clock restorer and a beautiful researcher cross paths at the grave of a long-dead British Army officer with a familiar name. His curiosity piqued, Alec 'Tick – Tock' Fraser joins a quest with Silvia on behalf of a wealthy Italian Count involving a roguish English baronet, a trip to New York and a priceless cello, all to unravel a mystery – what happened to the girl from Milan?

9 781916 095397